Kissed by Blood

The Sunwalker Saga, Prequel

Shéa MacLeod

Kissed by Blood
The Sunwalker Saga, Prequel
Text copyright © 2016 Shéa MacLeod
All rights reserved.
Printed in the United States of America.

Cover Art by Amanda Kelsey of Razzle Dazzle Designs
Editing by Theo Fenraven
Formatted by PyperPress

The characters and events portrayed in this book are fictitious. Any similarity to real persons, living or dead, is coincidental and not intended by the author.

Dedication

With great thanks to Sarah W. who suggested I tell the story of how Morgan became a hunter.

Shéa MacLeod

Prologue

Fangs gleamed wetly in the pale moonlight. My heart thudded in my chest as the vampire lowered his head. Bile rose in my throat as he inhaled deeply, like a cook sniffing a delicious stew. Bony fingers dug painfully into my shoulders as I fought him, twisting and turning. I lashed out until my foot connected with a kneecap. His leg buckled, but he didn't let go.

Red glowing eyes shot terror into my soul as sharp fangs drew ever closer to my bare throat. I scratched and tore at him but couldn't get loose. I felt helpless. I knew I was about to die.

Show him who you are.

The thought whispered through my mind. I had no idea what it meant, but I realized I was clutching something in my right hand. A stake, carved of wood, symbols etched in silver circling it. The vampire hadn't noticed it. I had one chance.

Gripping the stake, I drew back and drove it as hard as I could into the vampire's chest, right over his heart. He stared at me, surprised. His mouth opened, shut, and then between one breath and the next, he exploded into so much ash and dust.

I stood there beneath the half moon, the stake still clutched in my hand, staring at the pile of debris where a vampire had once stood. My shoulders still ached from his grip. No doubt there'd be bruises come morning.

"Morgan. Morgan Bailey, wake up right this minute. You're going to be late for school."

The blankets suddenly took flight, landing in a heap on my bedroom floor. The sudden cold air jarred me from sleep, dispersing the disturbing dream. I glared at my mother's retreating back as she disappeared out the door, footsteps receding down the short hall.

I rolled over and buried my face in the pillow. I was exhausted. My senior year of high school was the last thing on my mind at the moment. The dreams were getting weirder. If I wasn't careful, I was going to get sent to a shrink. Or worse, an exorcist.

"Morgan," my mother yelled from the kitchen, "get your backside out of bed, or I'm getting the ice water."

"I'm getting, I'm getting." With a muttered curse I staggered out of a cocoon of blankets and toward the bathroom. As I leaned over the sink brushing my teeth, I froze. On either shoulder were livid purple bruises in the shape of fingers.

Chapter 1

Seven Years Later

"Morgan, thank goodness, I need your help. It's an emergency." Arnoldo plopped his khaki-clad butt on my desk and gave me doe eyes from behind tortoiseshell glasses. His graying hair looked like he'd been running his hands through it again. It was a nervous habit of his. I snuck a look at the clock: 5:45 p.m. Of course he would wait until fifteen minutes before closing on a Friday to ask me to do some no doubt crucially important thing. He was a sweet man, though, so I didn't like to make a fuss.

"What is it, Arnoldo?" I gave him what I hoped was a patient smile when all I really wanted to do was grab my stuff and bolt.

"There is a conference next week in Milan. I need a flight, hotel, and the conference fee paid." He dropped a stack of paperwork on my desk. "Oh, and the conference application needs to be filled out. You don't mind, do you?" He beamed at me again.

I held back a sigh. "Sure. No problem." What else was I going to say? It was my job. Sort of. Not the filling out paperwork part, but certainly the acquiring tickets part. Unfortunately, I often found myself being talked into to doing things my coworkers should have done themselves. Liking the aforementioned paperwork.

He grinned. "I knew I could count on you. Have a good weekend." And with that he was out the door, coat in hand, probably off to enjoy a pint at the pub while I tried to make heads or tails of the mess he'd given me.

Don't get me wrong; I loved my job. Most of the time. But planning travel for other people had never been my life's dream. I wasn't sure what my life's dream was, but it had been more exciting, certainly. Still I couldn't complain. I lived in London, and how many Americans got to say that? It was like a dream come true.

It hadn't been my plan to live in London, either. Scotland, maybe. Or Paris, if I ever got the chance. Who doesn't dream of living in Paris?. But London? Not so much.

Things changed, though. The minute I set foot in London, I'd loved it with a passion that only those who have lived there could ever understand. My family certainly couldn't. My grandmother was sure I'd be murdered by redcoats. My grandmother tended toward the dramatic.

My mother was more worried I'd end up married and having babies with a Brit, which was, as far as she was concerned, a fate worse than murder at the hands of redcoats. I was supposed to get married and have babies and move into a house next door to her so she could see her grandchildren anytime she wanted. My moving halfway around the world was never part of her plan.

As for me, I didn't care what either of them thought. I was head over heels in love.

I'd met Alex at my local coffee shop in Portland, Oregon. He'd been on a business trip for a British antiques company and was in between client meetings. I'd sneaked out to grab a quick latte after my boss at the textile company where I was working then had berated me once again for something she'd done wrong. I'd needed the caffeine to steady my nerves.

Maybe it was his sexy British accent or his European charm, but from the moment we met, it felt like fate. I was sure it was "happily ever after." So when he asked me to move to England and marry him, I did it. I relocated to London, and there I stayed—even after I'd caught the bastard cheating on me two weeks before our wedding. Alex had had the gall to tell me he didn't love me anymore and, in fact, didn't even particularly like me. If there'd been signs early on, I'd been too naive to see them. Or maybe I'd seen them but had been too afraid to confront him. In any case, I was devastated.

Initially, I stayed in London because I didn't know what else to do. I thought if I stayed, Alex might realize he'd made a mistake and change his mind. Instead, I changed mine. I made friends, built a life, and enjoyed every minute of every day I lived in that most magical of cities.

I flipped through the stack of paperwork Arnoldo had given me. He'd filled out the personal information and some of the other stuff, but there was still a ton I'd have to do. It needed to be submitted right away. He was really cutting close to the wire. The hotel would probably already be booked. And the airlines... I shuddered to think what my boss would say about the cost of a last-minute flight to Milan.

It was almost seven by the time I finished. Having to work an hour late on a Friday made me grumpy, but I reminded myself to be grateful. At least I had a job, and in an amazing city, no less.

I was starving, so I sent a quick text to my friend, Clara, to see if she was up for dinner. She responded almost immediately with a suggestion to meet at Wahaca, a Mexican restaurant just down the street from my office. I'd always thought the name odd for a Mexican restaurant, until I realized it was the phonetic spelling of Oaxaca, one of Mexico's thirty-one states.

Snagging my red coat from the closet, I rushed out before I could get waylaid by anyone else. I desperately needed this weekend. Work had been hectic, and the dreams weren't helping.

I shook my head to clear it. I didn't want to think about the dreams. I don't know why I was having them now. They hadn't plagued me since I was a teenager, but now they were happening two or three times a week, each one more vivid and disturbing than the last.

Plunging into the cold of a London winter evening, I drew frigid air into my lungs. What I needed was a good, stiff drink. Or six. I needed to forget the disappointment that life wasn't quite as exciting as I'd hoped and focus on the good things.

Wahaca was a brisk ten-minute walk away. By the time I got there, my cheeks were pink, my eyes a little watery, and my nose running. Elegance, thy name is Morgan. Clara didn't notice. She was standing outside in a puffy, hot pink coat and painted on black jeans with rhinestones up the side seams. Her short, dark hair whipped wildly in the wind as she gave me a huge hug, exclaimed over how cute my new winter coat was, and dragged me inside.

The restaurant was perfumed with the scents of roasting meat, spicy chilies, and rich cheeses. My mouth watered, and my stomach gave a low rumble, masked by the bright, cheerful beat of merengue music. As we sipped margaritas at the bar, waiting for our table, I complained to Clara about having to work late.

"Girl, you gotta quit that place," she said, sipping her drink. She had salt on the rim of her glass. I'd asked for sugar on mine. It wasn't the "in" thing, but I've always preferred sweet to savory. "They don't value you properly, you know."

I sighed. "Maybe not, but the pay is decent, and the people are nice. Better than any place else I ever worked."

"They take advantage."

She had a point. I shrugged. "It's better than nothing, right? And I love that I get to work in Mayfair. It's so close to everything, and it makes it easier to hang out with you."

"That's true." She chinked her glass against mine. "Can't complain about that. But why don't you try something different? Booking travel for corporate wankers isn't exactly your life's goal, is it?"

"No. But I'm not sure what I want to do."

"In that case, let's have another." She waggled her empty margarita glass at the bartender. Within seconds we both had fresh drinks. Double shots. Clara raised her glass. "Here's to finding your passion."

I grinned. "I'll drink to that."

# # #

As usual, when hanging with Clara, I drank more than I should have, but the margaritas went down easily, and I'd had a long day. Longer than it should have been, thanks to Arnoldo. He was a nice man, but he could try my patience. His long-suffering wife agreed with me apparently. She occasionally baked me cookies or muffins and delivered them with an apologetic smile. Bless her.

The Oxford Circus Tube Station was a short walk from Wahaca, back in the direction of my office. Chill wind whipped at my coat hem as I strode quickly along, feeling the warm, fuzzy detachment brought about by too much tequila.

The bright fluorescent lights of the station beckoned me closer. Exhaustion pressed on me even through the alcohol fog. I wanted nothing more than to get home to my flannel pajamas, warm bed, and something mind-numbing on the telly. Ahead of me a couple walked arm in arm, heads close together as if they shared a world of secrets. A pang of jealously, ruthlessly quashed, stirred inside me.

I stumbled to a halt as a bone-chilling scream ripped through the air. Heart lodging in my throat, I glanced wildly around, trying to find the source of the scream. Nothing. And the couple seemingly hadn't noticed. They kept walking toward the station, laughing softly over some private joke.

Swallowing hard, I cinched the belt of my coat tighter and picked up the pace. The safety of the station was half a block away. Somehow I felt I'd be safe inside from whatever had screamed. Or whatever had made the person scream. I shivered, the tequila warmth suddenly dissipated.

A woman brushed by me, startling me so badly, I nearly tripped over my own feet. She glanced behind her, her dark cloud of hair whipping wildly in the wind. Dark eyes snared me, chilling me to the bone. Did I know her? She seemed familiar, if a bit scary.

A small smile quirked her wide lips. "Pardon." She muttered the usual British apology, and then she was gone, slipping away from the lights of the station and disappearing into the night.

I stood for what seemed forever, frozen in place. Why had the strange woman affected me so? I shrugged it off, telling myself not to be an idiot, but I took the rest of the way to the station at nearly a full run.

Shéa MacLeod

Chapter 2

Monday my train was delayed. I was a full fifteen minutes late to work. I needn't have worried. No one was at their desks. Instead they huddled around the television set in the breakroom, muttering to each other.

"What's going on?" I asked Ana, the girl standing closest to the coffee pot as I poured myself a cup and doctored the brown stuff liberally with milk and sugar. The Brits didn't believe in cream. It was scandalous, if you asked me, but I'd managed to adapt. More or less.

Ana swept a lock of black hair out of her eyes. "You won't believe it, Morgan. The most awful thing."

"Yeah, so I gathered." I tried standing on tiptoe so I could see over everyone's heads, but it was no use. "Spill."

"There's been"—she paused for dramatic effect—"a *murder.*"

"Oh." It wasn't that I meant to sound so disappointed, but this was London. Murders weren't unheard of. In a city of over eight and a half million people, death was bound to happen.

"No, you don't understand." She grabbed my arm, her

eyes wide with excitement. "The body... it was drained of all blood." In her excitement, Ana's Brazilian accent grew thicker than usual. "And there were holes in her throat. Two of them." She pointed to her own throat. "I think it was a vampire." She pronounced it "vum-PIRE," which made the word sound almost cute.

I held back a snort of laughter. She seemed serious, but the idea was ludicrous. "There are no such things as vampires."

"No?" She crossed her arms and gave me a stubborn look. "Who says?"

"Everyone sane. It's probably just some crazy person trying to throw off the cops or something." I started to turn away.

She snorted. "This is not the first time."

I turned back slowly. "What?"

She gave me a smug smile, thrilled she had information I didn't. She leaned forward, practically oozing with excitement. "Last week there was this woman. They found her in a park. Same thing. No blood and two holes in her throat."

Surely not a coincidence. Serial killer, maybe? "What does the news say?"

Ana waved one hand in annoyance. "Not much. You

know these people. Lots of talk, no information. But let me tell you"—she leaned closer—"sure as I stand here, it's a vampire. You'll see."

I took a sip of my coffee. "Okay then. I'm going to work. Let me know if there are any more vampire attacks, will you?"

"You mock, but you'll see." She arched her eyebrow at me. "Then I will say 'I told you so.'"

I grinned. "And I'll deserve it. I'll even buy you a hot chocolate."

"Hell, no. You'll buy me a proper drink."

I laughed. "It's a deal."

As I walked back to my desk, I thought about Ana's vampire story. The whole thing was absurd, but I couldn't help remembering the scream I'd heard Friday night and the mysterious woman who'd bumped into me.

At my desk, I pulled up a news article on the murder. I quickly scanned the article, stumbling to a halt as I read: ... although the body was found this morning, police believe the victim was murdered Friday night...

My blood ran cold as I stared at the words over and over. In my mind, I could still hear the scream.

# # #

That night, walking to Bond Street Tube Station, I couldn't help feeling uneasy. Every shadow seemed alive. Every dark doorway held danger. It was ridiculous. I'd always felt safe on the streets of London, particularly in Mayfair. Not tonight. Tonight I couldn't get my mind off the news story and Ana's nutty conspiracy theory.

Of course, the very idea of vampires was preposterous. No such thing. Everyone knew that. But someone playing at vampire? That was another story. Some nut with a blood fetish, no doubt. I'd seen a special about it on one of the documentary channels.

I shivered, drawing deeper into my coat and snugging my scarf more securely around my neck. It was silly. A scarf would never stop a serial killer.

Something metallic skittered in the darkness, like someone had kicked a tin can. I stumbled to a stop, my heart rate kicking into full gear. I strained to see into the shadows of the alley across the street. I was sure the sound had come from there, but I couldn't see anything. The weak golden glow of the streetlamps was warm and cheery but no good for seeing into dark places.

The sound came again, followed by a grunt, and my flight impulse kicked in. I didn't run exactly, more like fast-walked down the nearly deserted street. Just two more blocks, and I could turn the corner. The station would be right there, half a block from the corner, bright lights spilling onto the street and a never-ending stream of humanity parading in and out. Whatever was going on in that alley wasn't my business. And it probably wasn't the vampire killer anyway. Why would he, or she, be running around Mayfair?

I was steps from the corner when a voice spoke so close to my ear, I nearly jumped out of my skin.

"Excuse me. I believe you dropped this."

I spun around, arms raised as if to ward off an attack. I found myself facing a woman about three inches shorter than me. Her wild, curly hair seemed to soak up the light, it was so black. I recognized her instantly. It was the woman who'd slammed into me outside Wahaca Friday night. Was she following me? I laughed at myself for being ridiculous. She probably lived around here. Life was funny like that. You never saw a person before and then suddenly you were running into them everywhere.

"Here," she said, thrusting her hand at me. In it was a knit glove. It was definitely mine. I hadn't even realized I'd dropped it. It had probably fallen out of my pocket.

"Um, thanks," I said, taking it from her and stuffing it

in a pocket. "No problem." She gave me a wide smile, showing off perfect rows of pearly white teeth. "You should be more careful."

"I will," I assured her, fidgeting awkwardly with my purse strap.

With a nod, she turned and strode away. I had the oddest feeling she hadn't been talking about me losing my glove.

Chapter 3

The Tube was crowded, people standing literally nose to armpit in the steamy car. It was one of the miseries of London a person just put up with. I tried to leave work at less congested travel times, but sometimes there was nothing for it. You just had to put up.

The car swayed, jerking us riders like we were on a theme park ride. I slammed against the solid chest of a neatly dressed young man. We murmured apologies to each other as we extricated ourselves from the embarrassing encounter. Actually, he seemed more embarrassed than I was. Maybe it was my American-ness. Things like this didn't much phase me. I didn't seem to need quite as much personal space as most British did.

The car gave another jerk, this time in the opposite direction, sending me reeling back into a middle-aged woman clutching half a dozen shopping bags. More apologies followed. I felt bad I'd crumpled her fancy bags, but what kind of idiot went shopping at the busiest transit time of the day?

As I got myself upright, something caught the corner of my eye. I jerked my head to the left, trying to catch another glimpse, sure I was mistaken. I couldn't have seen what I thought I had. Must have been my overactive imagination.

I squeezed my eyes shut and opened them again, craning my neck in the direction I'd seen… it. There it was, plain as day and twice as mean. I drew in a shaky breath, gripping the yellow pole until my knuckles turned white.

"You all right, miss?"

I glanced up. An elderly Sikh man with a blue turban leaned over me with troubled eyes. I must have looked a fright. Most people don't talk to anyone on the Tube, even if they looked like they were dying, but his accent marked him a foreigner, like me. Maybe he hadn't been here long enough to know the unwritten rules.

I swallowed. "I'm all right. Just a bit dizzy."

"Oh, yes, these rides are something awful, no? Just take deep breaths, and you will be fine, I assure you."

I gave him a weak smile. "Thanks. Do you, ah, see that person over there in the purple coat?"

He looked to where I indicated. "The young woman? Do you know her?"

"She looks familiar, is all. I thought maybe she was a celebrity. They ride the tubes sometimes, you know."

"Do they?" His eyes lit up. "How exciting."

He said something else, but I wasn't listening because he saw a young woman, but I saw something totally different. I might be losing my mind, but I was pretty sure the person in the purple coat was a demon.

# # #

I didn't tell anyone what I'd seen on the Tube. No doubt they'd think I'd lost my ever-loving mind. Ana might buy it, but she'd be the only one. Everyone else would kindly suggest a trip to the psychiatrist. Maybe I did need to see a doctor. I hadn't seen anything like that in years, and then only in dreams.

The week trudged along with its usual slow drudgery, the days broken only by multiple trips to the breakroom for heavenly Brazilian coffee and lunches at the pub with various workmates. In the evening I'd slip out of the office a few minutes before six so Arnoldo couldn't catch me again. Every time I entered the Tube Station, I'd brace myself, waiting for a glimpse of either the mysterious dark-haired woman or the demon girl. I saw neither.

Thursday finally came to an end, and I breathed a sigh of relief. Only Friday left before another weekend. I had no plans, but it didn't matter. Just getting away from the office for a couple days was a relief.

Usually I walked the mile home through the park, but it was cold and dark and I was exhausted, so I hopped onto the bus for the short ride from the station. From the bus stop, home was a few blocks away. I shivered in the chill, wishing I had remembered to bring a hat.

Autumn leaves crunched softly underfoot, and the faint scent of wood smoke tickled my nose. I forced my shoulders to relax as I inhaled the crisp October air. From up on Headstone Road came the steady hum of rush-hour traffic, but my street was quiet, all my neighbors shut up in their homes for hot dinners and an evening in front of the telly. I tugged my scarf a little higher around my throat and tucked my hands deep into the pockets of my wool coat.

I walked a little faster. My flat would be nice and warm, and an evening of sci-fi and crime shows sounded fantastic. I spotted the red-and-white brick of my building through the bushes. I fumbled for my keys, which had managed to lose themselves once again inside the depths of my handbag.

Something heavy slammed into my left side. I flew through the air and smashed into my neighbor's stonework wall. I actually heard my own ribs snap. The pain made me gag.

I never even saw it coming, and my mind struggled to make sense of the fact that I was now lying on the freezing cold ground, feeling like I'd been rammed by a truck. Making a little mewling sound in my throat, I groped for my handbag. Everything had spilled out across the pavement. My fingers skittered across lipstick tubes and pens. My phone. Where was it? I needed to call... someone.

I saw it lying about a foot away. I reached for it, but the pain in my side was overwhelming. I couldn't even cry, I hurt so badly.

I glanced up and down the street, looking for help, and realized my vision had gone fuzzy. I tasted blood in my mouth. I reached up and touched my right temple and cheek where I'd hit the wall. My fingers came away sticky with blood. My stomach pitched.

Gods, what had hit me? A car, maybe? But all the cars along the street were parked and empty. I couldn't see anything else, just an empty street in front of me and the cold stone wall behind me.

"Help." It was hardly more than a whisper. I tried again. "Help!" It didn't come out much louder, but someone heard me because behind me, there was a low laugh in response. My blood ran cold. Fear clawed at my insides, screaming at me to get up and run.

"No one gonna help you, bitch. No one gonna hear you." The speaker moved around and crouched down beside me.

I blinked to clear my vision and wished I hadn't. Nightmares were prettier. His face was hollow looking, waxy pale skin sunken against his skull. Yellowish fangs extended past his lower lip like a freak out of some horror movie.

I thought I must have hit my head harder than I realized. I tried to push myself to my feet, but I cried out as another wave of pain hit me.

He laughed, and when he did, those long fangs flashed in the amber light of the streetlamp. If it weren't for the agony, I would have thought I was dreaming. They didn't exist. Vampires weren't real.

I felt the fangs go right into my jugular. It hurt more than anything. The pain ripped through me worse than the broken ribs or the head trauma. I would have screamed, but I had no breath. My hands fluttered against him, trying to beat him off, but I had no strength. His clawed hands squeezed my throat shut, and he slammed my head into the wall again.

There was only the sound of my heart beating slower and slower and slower. Then it stopped. The world went black, and there was no more pain and no more blood and no more fear.

Shéa MacLeod

Chapter 4

I blinked against a world of harsh, bright white. The sheets beneath my fingertips felt cool and smooth and smelled faintly of bleach. The light stabbed viciously though my head, as if the light was solid shards, lodging a violent ache behind my eyes. I squinted, trying to filter the glare.

I obviously wasn't dead. Wasn't sure whether to be relieved or not.

I ran a quick mental check. Other than the headache, nothing hurt, which could be a good sign or a very bad one. I subtly flexed my muscles and bent my joints, starting from the toes and moving up. Mostly everything worked, except I was strapped to the bed with thick leather cuffs. That baffled me. I was the victim here. I was the one who'd been attacked. Didn't they know that? Why was I tied down?

I must have made a noise, because a face came into view, hovering over my bed. Dark eyes and honey-kissed cinnamon skin, an expression far too serious for a face meant to smile at the world. She looked familiar. "How are you feeling?" The woman had an accent that wasn't quite British but close.

"Um, okay, I think." I frowned trying to figure out where I'd seen her before. "How long have I been out?"

"Three days."

I stared at her. Three days? How was that even possible?

"You were banged up pretty bad," she said, as if reading my mind. Her voice was cool, detached, her eyes watchful, as if I might morph into an alien right in front of her. What was her deal, anyway?

My mouth tasted of road kill and felt stuffed full of cotton. I cleared my throat, wishing for some water. "Thank God. I thought I died."

Her smile turned strangely tender. "Yeah," she said softly, "you did."

I froze. My heartbeat seemed to slow before kicking into high gear, thundering in my ears. My voice was so faint, I was surprised she heard me. "Excuse me?"

"You heard me."

"I don't understand." An edge of panic creeped into my voice.

"You will."

"What does that mean?" I wanted to scream or shake her or something.

She didn't answer, which I found not only annoying but downright scary.

"Don't I know you?" I eyed her closely. A thought wormed its way into my pounding head. "You're the woman from the alley. The one who returned my glove. Are you following me?"

"In a manner of speaking. But it was for your own protection."

Fat lot of good that had done. My voice came out a raspy whisper. "What is that supposed to mean?"

"In time."

I all but growled in frustration. This runaround business was beyond irritating. "Why am I cuffed to the bed?"

"Just in case." She pulled a chair up and leaned over to rest her elbows on her knees. Her pose was casual, but every muscle was tensed.

"In case of what?" The image of the creature who'd attacked me flooded my mind, turning my voice a bit shrill. Fear clawed at the back of my throat. I wanted to believe I'd imagined the whole thing, but I knew I hadn't. What I'd seen shouldn't exist, but it did. I knew what I'd seen was true. Just like the demon on the train.

I remembered the fangs ripping into my throat, the

pain, the blood, the sharp stink of fear. My fear. I'd felt my life ebbing away, leaking out onto the cold pavement. I should have been dead. The refrain kept pounding through my head: *I should be dead.*

"In case you turn." Her voice was flat.

"Turn? Turn into what?" Panic tried to take hold, but I fought it down with a fierceness I didn't know I had.

"A vampire."

"Are you serious?" This had to be some kind of joke. It was like a bad science fiction movie.

She wasn't kidding. "We tied you down in case you turn into a vampire. It's what happens when those things bite you." I could tell by her expression that if I had turned, we wouldn't be having this conversation.

"I didn't turn." I wanted to feel relieved, but I didn't. Not yet. Not until I was sure. Another thought struck me. "Wait. Vampires are real?" What I'd seen already told me they were real, but I wanted someone to confirm I wasn't crazy, and this mysterious woman was the only one here.

This time her smile was pure and true. "Yes, vampires are real. So are a lot of other nasty things you've probably never heard of." She eyed me. "And maybe some you have."

I didn't even want to know what she meant by "other

nasty things." I was still trying to get over the fact that vampires were not only real, but they weren't the dazzling, beautiful creatures of Hollywood. The creature that had attacked me had been anything but sexy, and he certainly hadn't been interested in anything but ripping my throat out. "Why didn't I turn? I mean, if that's what's supposed to happen." It all seemed so unreal. Maybe I was still unconscious and having a nightmare.

She shrugged. "I still don't know. If you were going to turn, you should have done it within the first twenty-four hours."

I breathed a sigh of relief. "Thank the gods."

"Yeah, you should definitely be thanking somebody. Nobody survives a vampire attack like that without turning. Nobody. "Her eyes narrowed as she eyeballed me. I didn't know what her problem was. Wasn't like it was my fault. "Every single attack victim we've found has died and turned. You're the first who hasn't, and we don't know why. Do you?"

"No. I don't." Why would I? The very idea was ludicrous.

She looked me over as though I were an interesting new specimen. Despite my fear and bewilderment, I refused to squirm.

"Good, you'll do." Her expression went from cool curiosity to warm approval that fast. It threw me a little, but it also made me feel kind of warm and fuzzy inside. Acceptance always felt good, even when you didn't know why you were being accepted.

I gave her a baffled look. I was feeling decidedly confused and a little bit lost. "Do for what?"

She stripped off the binding on my wrists, then stuck her hand out. I took it gingerly, and she gave my hand a firm shake. "I'm Kabita Jones, vampire hunter and demon slayer. Welcome to my world, Morgan Bailey."

# # #

Getting out of the hospital was relatively easy. I was all for waiting for the doctor to release me and walking out like a normal person, but Kabita insisted we were being watched and needed to sneak away. It sounded nuts to me, but whatever. This whole entire day, week, month was one for the books.

My clothes had been covered in blood and ripped to shreds, so Kabita brought me a pair of jeans, a black T-shirt, and a gray hoodie. As I stepped into the jeans, I pondered what Kabita had told me. The whole vampire/demon slaying thing? Totally ludicrous.

Except I'd been seeing demons since before I'd graduated high school. Like the one on the Tube the other night. And then there were the dreams. Dreams that had plagued me since childhood. Dreams about battling vampires and other monsters. At one point my mother had even sent me to a child psychologist, who'd listened to my latest dream, blanched white, then told my mother it was "perfectly normal," and my psyche was just trying to "work out a place in the world" or some stupid psychobabble. My mother had bought it. Me, not so much. Even at five I was a skeptic.

Still, this whole escaping-from-the-hospital-because-bad-people-are-watching thing was a bit over the top. I pulled the T-shirt over my head and zipped up the hoodie. I couldn't imagine who on earth would care I'd survived or that I was leaving the hospital.

"Did you tell my mother?" I asked as I searched for shoes. Kabita hadn't brought me any, but the black ballet flats I'd been wearing when they brought me in were sitting in a cupboard. As far as I could tell, there wasn't any blood on them, so I slipped them on with a shrug. Better than nothing.

"That you were technically dead? No. She has no idea

anything happened to you at all. As far as she's concerned, life has been normal the past three days."

"How'd you manage that?" If I didn't check in with her at least every other day, my mother had a tendency to freak out.

Kabita gave me a wry look. "Your email wasn't that hard to hack."

"You hacked my email?" I half screeched.

One eyebrow went up. "You wanted her to panic?"

She had a point. I nodded in relief. "What about my friends? Work?"

"I pretended to be your roommate and called in sick for you. Told them you had laryngitis. The only friend who texted was someone called Clara. Gave her the same line." She stuck her head out the door to check if the coast was clear. "Ready?" she asked, glancing at me.

"As I'll ever be. Is this really necessary?"

She gave me a look. One that said "don't mess with me." "Trust me."

"Okay." What else could I do? If she was right, I'd been bitten by a freaking vampire. I'd died and come back. It was creepy as hell. But I knew something really bad had happened, and I'd survived. I knew I'd been badly injured, yet my body didn't have a mark on it. I wasn't even sore, and I should have been. That freaked me out as much as anything.

I slipped out the door to join her in the hallway. It was quiet enough, I could hear the murmur of voices from the nurses' station around the corner. Somebody was watching *Strictly Come Dancing* —the original UK version of *Dancing with the Stars*—somewhere down the hall. Otherwise everything was still. At the end of the hall, a window showed it was dark outside.

"This way," Kabita hissed, motioning me to the stairwell. I made my way toward her, trying to move as noiselessly as possible. Believe me, I didn't come close to her level of stealth. She rolled her eyes. "Hurry up, would you?"

With a shrug, I ran down the hall and squeezed past her into the stairwell. "Sorry. I was trying to be quiet."

She snorted. "Good luck with that. Guess that'll be first on your list of lessons."

Lessons? I was getting lessons? I opened my mouth to ask about them, but she shushed me.

"Let's get out of here first, then we can talk."

I nodded reluctantly. I still thought this whole stealth escape thing was unnecessary, but I was going along with it because I was curious and also because of those dreams. I needed to know how real they'd been, and somehow I knew Kabita Jones was the person to tell me.

We finally hit the ground floor, and Kabita held up a hand, indicating we should stop. She gripped the crash bar with one hand and pulled out a wicked looking blade with the other.

"What the—"

She shot me a glare. I shut my mouth. Right. Questions later. Like how the hell she'd gotten a knife like that into the hospital in the first place, and why she felt the need to carry it in the second. Lord, what had I gotten myself into?

The vamps hit the minute she opened the door, coming at us from both sides. As I went down in a heap under the weight of the first one, Kabita's blade flashed in the light of a nearby streetlamp. My last thought as I hit the ground was I hoped she got to me before I ended up dead. Again.

Chapter 5

"Get up." Kabita loomed over me like an avenging angel. She was wearing all black, so I couldn't see the blood, but there were dark stains on her knife so I was pretty sure there'd been a lot of it.

As I stood, I patted myself down, checking for fang marks. Or whatever.

She sighed in exasperation and shoved a lock of dark, wavy hair out of her face. "You're fine. You banged your head a bit, but the vamp didn't bite you. Not that it would matter." She muttered the last under her breath.

"What does that mean?"

"You're immune to vamp bites."

"Um, yay?" I remembered the flash of elongated fang. The hideous face looming above me. And the breath, like something from the grave. Yuck. "Those were vampires?"

"Yes." She said it like most people would say "duh." She whirled and strode toward the car park, me trotting along behind her like a good little minion. She stopped in front of a black SUV and hit the key fob. I heard the snap of the lock, and it jarred me from my fugue.

My mind was swirling like so much glitter down a

toilet. This was crazy. This whole thing was nuts. Vampires? Who the fuck believed in vampires? Nobody sane, that's who. I was not about to get into a car with a crazy woman.

Kabita climbed into the driver's seat, then rolled down the passenger window. "Get in," she snapped like a drill sergeant.

I backed away slowly, shaking my head. "No. No way. This is crazy. I am not getting in that car with you. You could be the serial killer for all I know."

She rolled her eyes. "Morgan, I explained—"

"No!" I cut her off. "You're insane if you think I'm going to buy this nonsense. Just... leave me alone." I whirled and ran from the car park as fast as I could. The vehicle's engine revved behind me, and I ran faster, tearing past rows of neatly parked cars, their colorful paint jobs shining beneath the dull lighting.

I was nearly to the entrance when Kabita pulled up alongside me. I half expected her to jump out of the car and wrestle me to the ground, but she didn't. Instead she threw something out the window. "Call me when you come to your senses." Then she tore out of the car park with a screech of tires.

On the ground lay a small white card. I couldn't help

myself. I leaned down and picked it up. On it was a number. Nothing else. I crumpled it up. No way was I calling her. I strode toward the nearest rubbish bin, my hand hovering over the opening. Something stopped me. Instead of throwing the card away, I stuffed it in my pocket. Just in case.

#

"Girl, what are you wearing?" Clara asked as she plopped down on the bench beside me. It was a chilly day, and it was all I could do to stop my teeth chattering. I was not dressed for this weather. Clara looked warm and cozy in her thick, quilted jacket, and wool hat and mittens. "If you've been sick, you should wear something more..."—she gestured wildly—"Wintery."

"Rumors of my illness are vastly exaggerated," I said.

"Your flatmate told me you were in hospital. Don't tell me it wasn't serious."

"I'm all right now, but, ah, I have a small problem."

"What is it? I'll help. Whatever you need."

I managed a smile. I knew I could count on Clara. "In the hospital there was sort of a mix-up. Um, my clothes were ruined. I have no idea where my purse and stuff are.

My phone is gone." That was probably the most annoying thing of all. "Oyster card, too, which is why I can't take the Tube. Keys are gone. Obviously my debit and credit cards are gone, and I can't go into the bank to get new ones, looking like this. I haven't had a shower in three days."

"A mix-up? You ought to sue. I tell you, people just don't take responsibility. I could give you money for a ticket. Surely your flatmate will let you in."

I shifted uncomfortably. "I'm scared to go home," I admitted.

She looked confused. "Scared?"

"What if I have a, ah, relapse or something?"

She nodded sagely. "Don't worry, you come home with me. Take a shower. Get some rest. You can stay as long as you like, and we'll get you some new things. Everything can be replaced."

That was easy for her to say. She wasn't the one who was homeless, clothes-less, and being chased by monsters. She wasn't the one who'd met a crazy woman in the hospital and been told vampires were real.

Hallucination. That's what it was. I'd bumped my head and hallucinated the whole thing. Vampires weren't real. Kabita Jones was a figment of my overactive imagination.

I hadn't died at all. I'd just been in a coma or something. That was it. Everything was fine now. Or it would be.

The minute we got to her flat, Clara handed me the phone to call my bank and cancel my cards. It was surprisingly easy. They told me I could pick up my new ones at the nearby branch in a couple of days.

Next, I called my boss to let her know I was on the mend. Fortunately, she was very excited to hear I was getting better and encouraged me to take the rest of the week off and she'd see me Monday. It was a relief. My life would soon be back to normal.

# # #

Fangs flashed in the moonlight, dripping long strands of bloody saliva. Eyes filled with madness glared into my own, and my soul shriveled up inside me. The fangs flashed again, and this time I felt sharp pain as they sank into my tender neck. I tried to scream, but my throat filled with blood...

I came awake, thrashing at the duvet and screaming incoherently. The light snapped on, and Clara stood in the doorway dressed in leopard print pajamas.

"Morgan? What happened?"

I sighed and flopped back on the pillow. "Another nightmare." I'd been at Clara's three days now, and every night had been plagued with nightmares, each worse than the last. I wanted to go home, but I was afraid the vampires knew where I lived. What if I was attacked again? This time I might not survive.

Clara padded over and sat on the edge of the narrow guest bed. "Girl, you gotta see somebody about this. They're getting worse."

I felt bad. Every time I had one, I woke her up. She had to be sick and tired of me by now. I nodded. "I will. First thing in the morning."

She nodded. "Cup of tea?"

I shook my head and gave her a wry smile. "No thanks. I'll be fine."

Clara shrugged as if to say "suit yourself" and headed back to bed. I waited until I heard her door click shut and then I opened the nightstand drawer. Inside were various bits and pieces I'd collected in the last few days. I dug around until I found what I was looking for: a small, crumpled white card with a string of numbers on it. It was time to make that call.

Chapter 6

I expected Kabita to gloat. She didn't. In fact, her expression didn't change at all. She merely pulled up to the curb, reached over and unlocked the door, then waited while I climbed in. She was silent as she pulled back into traffic.

Finally I couldn't stand it anymore. "You're probably wondering why I called," I blurted.

"Figured it was the nightmares."

I blinked. "Excuse me? How do you know about those?"

She shrugged. "You don't deal with reality, your brain is going to have a meltdown. It's how dreams work." As if it made total sense.

"No. No. I refuse to accept this." I gripped the edge of my seat so hard, my knuckles turned white.

"You don't have a choice."

I nearly growled. "There are no such things as vampires."

She was silent, simply waiting.

"I'm not this person you think I am. I'm not part of your world."

No answer. Just eyes straight ahead, focused on the road.

I let out a scream of frustration. "This can't be real. It's...nuts."

"That it is," she agreed. There was a pause. "I can see how this might be difficult for you, being new to such things, but denying reality won't make it go away. I've been experiencing this my entire life. It is what it is and pretending different won't make it so. You're a hunter, Morgan, whether you like it or not."

I stared glumly out the window. She was right, of course, but I was still having a hard time believing this was real, that I wasn't still in a coma in the hospital having a very weird dream.

We drove out to the edge of London. Shops and houses gave way to empty warehouses. Kabita pulled up in front of one of the buildings. It was two stories, brick, with a long loading dock out front.

"This is it," she said.

I frowned. "This is what?"

"My place."

"You live here?" I asked, surprised.

She nodded. "On the upper floor. Training room is in the basement. You'll stay here, too. I'll arrange to have your things brought over." She opened the door and climbed out.

I scrambled to follow suit. "Excuse me?"

She turned and gave me a look. "You want my help or not?"

I sighed. "Of course I do. But you can't just—"

"Then you'll stay here and train with me."

"Why me?" I doubted I was the first to ask her that question. Likely wouldn't be the last.

An even longer pause. "Why not you?"

# # #

"And again. Harder this time. Punch like you're going to shove your fist right through his face and out the other side."

I grimaced at the image. *Gross.* But I did what she said. I pretended the punching bag was a vampire, and I was slamming my fist literally through his head. I punched. The bag exploded, sand sprayed everywhere, and Kabita got a face full.

She choked and coughed as she brushed herself off. "Excellent," she said dryly

I stared at the remains of the bag swinging limply from

its chain. "What the hell?" Seriously, I'm a mega-wuss. I'd be more likely to break my hand than bust a punching bag, yet it dangled sadly, like a balloon that had lost its air.

"I told you. You're a hunter. Thanks to a quirk of genetics, you're now stronger and faster than you were before. Stronger and faster than most humans, in fact."

I narrowed my gaze. "Like, I have superpowers or something?"

"Or something. You can't stop bullets or fangs, though, so don't be an idiot." She stabbed her forefinger in the direction of a second bag. "Let's go again."

So I did. And another innocent sandbag lost the will to live.

"Again," Kabita said, marching toward a third bag.

"Really?" At this rate we were going to run out of sandbags.

"Yes, really," she said, crossing her arms and tapping her foot impatiently.

"Isn't it enough I destroyed two bags? It's obvious I've got this down."

She sighed heavily. "You've got the power, but your technique is off. Now punch the bag."

I spent the next twenty minutes destroying the last three bags. I figured surely she'd let me stop. I figured wrong.

"We'll practice again tomorrow. It's time to learn to use a sword."

I frowned. "What for? This isn't medieval England."

"And yet swords come in immensely useful when removing a vampire's head."

"Ew." I shuddered. "You do that?"

"Not if I can help it. I'm not a vampire hunter. That's your job."

I made a gagging motion. "That's disgusting."

"Get over it. It'll save your life one day."

She really had zero sympathy. Did she not understand what I was going through? I'd only just discovered I was some weird hunter—something I wasn't sure I totally bought despite the punching bag evidence—and now I was being faced with the proposition of chopping off heads . Seriously, it was so messed up. And definitely not legal. My mother would be horrified.

Still, when she handed me a carved wooden sword, I took it. "What's this?"

"Practice sword. I'd rather my own head stayed attached, thank you." Her tone was tart.

I snickered, although I was a tad disappointed. It would have been kind of cool to wield a real sword like the Knights of the Round Table.

Kabita showed me the finer points of holding a sword properly. By the time she finished, my arm ached from holding the damn thing up, and we hadn't even gotten to the actual fighting. I may have had superpowers now, if Kabita and the dead sandbags were to be believed, but my muscles hadn't gotten the memo.

"Most vamps won't be carrying swords," Kabita said, interrupting my thoughts. "Or likely any other weapon. They rely almost entirely on fangs and claws."

"Vampires have claws?" Not quite what they showed in the movies.

"Not true claws, but very long, very sharp fingernails. Believe me, they might as well be claws."

"Well, then, killing one ought to be easy. Flick of the sword,"—I demonstrated rather sloppily, and my arm protested the movement—"and you've got a dead vampire. Easy peasy."

She snorted. "Oh, you think so? Try this on for size. As fast and strong as you are, a vamp is faster, stronger, and a hell of a lot meaner. You care about survival. About playing fair and doing the right thing. They care about nothing but ripping you to shreds and sucking the blood from your veins."

"Oh, goody," I said lightly, but my stomach churned.

"Do you want to learn?" she snapped. "Or would you rather stand here and be snarky? Hope for the best next time you're attacked?"

My eyes widened. "Next time?"

She threw back her head and laughed. It was a harsh, grating sound, like she hadn't done it in a while. "You think you're out of the woods, kid?" Who was she calling "kid?" She was barely older than me. "Let me clue you in. You're a hunter now. You've got a big red bullseye on your back. From now on, every vamp from here to Hadrian's Wall will be out for your blood, and you'd better know how to protect yourself, or you're going to be dinner."

"Oh, goody." This time I didn't say it lightly at all.

# # #

The days passed more or less the same. Straight after breakfast, Kabita would march me down to the basement gym. I'd destroy no less than half a dozen punching bags before being allowed into the "ring."

Basically, the ring looked like a boxing ring except instead of boxing gloves, we armed ourselves with wooden practice swords. Then we'd spend hours circling, stabbing, slashing, and whatever else Kabita dreamed up until she'd finally call it quits, and I'd drag my exhausted ass from the gym, bruised from head to toe. Of course, the bruises were always gone by morning thanks to my new hunter speed-healing, but that didn't make them hurt any less.

I tried to keep my job at first, but between the travel and hours of training, it got to be too much. I finally gave in to Kabita's urging and quit. I'd also packed up my stuff, put it in storage, and moved into the warehouse. I almost never went out anymore. I still got the occasional texts and whatnot from friends, but I was always having to turn them down, which led to fewer and fewer invites. The whole thing was vaguely depressing, but I tried not to think about it.

The dreams had abated, however, which was a relief. Apparently embracing my inner hunter was all it had taken.

I was about three weeks in and nursing my second cup of coffee, hunched over the tiny table tucked into the corner of the eat-in kitchen. Usually by now Kabita would be haranguing me to finish up and get my ass to the gym, but this morning she was nowhere to be seen. Or heard, for that matter.

I frowned as I rinsed out the plain, black mug and set it to dry on the dish drainer. Maybe this was some kind of test? Kabita liked to pull shit like that. To "prepare" me, or so she claimed. Maybe she was already down in the gym, waiting to pounce on me and chew my ass out for being late.

Still feeling groggy and grumpy, I went to the stairwell and hurried downstairs. The basement door, usually left open for fresh air, was closed. That was odd but nothing that concerned me terribly. I turned the handle and pushed the door open as quietly as possible. Kabita didn't notice. She was on the phone, pacing back and forth with a scowl plastered on her face. "Are you sure?" she snapped. Whoever it was must have answered in the affirmative because she breathed a heartfelt, "Shit." Unusual for her. I'd noticed that, unlike me, Kabita rarely swore. When she did, I knew it was trouble.

"How many?" she was asking the person on the other end of the line. There was a pause and then, "You're kidding me." She rubbed the bridge of her nose tiredly. "How have the police missed this? The dead bodies are practically piling up."

Dead bodies? Was she talking about vampires or their

51

victims?

"You're sure it's connected to Morgan?"

My ears perked up. What now? I moved cautiously behind one of the punching bags, hoping Kabita wouldn't notice and would spill more interesting information.

"What's your plan? Uh-huh. Okay. Yeah, I got it. Later." The conversation cut off abruptly, and she shoved the phone in her pocket. "You can come out now."

Well, crap. I guess I wasn't as stealthy as I'd thought. "What's connected to me?" I figured if I was somehow involved in something, I had a right to know.

Kabita heaved a heavy sigh. "There have been several attacks in recent weeks on women throughout London. A few men, too. All the attacks have been carried out by vampires. We believe they are connected to the attack on you, the one that put you in hospital."

I blinked. "Why would the attacks be connected to me? I'm sure vampires have gone after a lot of people over the years."

She frowned. "Yes, but these were all potential hunters."

"Excuse me?"

"Remember I told you it was a genetic anomaly that allowed you to survive the attack, right? The same anomaly is what allowed you to transition into a hunter."

I nodded. "Okay."

"Well, all these people had a similar genetic anomaly. Had they survived, they would have developed the same hunter abilities you have."

"A *similar* genetic anomaly? What's that supposed to mean? Why didn't they survive?" I asked.

"Because in each case, the vampire ripped out the victim's heart."

I swallowed back bile. "But not me."

"No," she said grimly. "I believe the vampire who attacked you was interrupted."

By a couple of paramedics on their dinner break. I'd survived because of a fluke, not genetics. A sudden chill passed through me.

"Who is doing this? Why?"

"We don't know," she said with a shake of her head. "Clearly someone is out to destroy potential hunters. Why, we don't know, but there is an architect here, someone directing the vamps' attacks. The people I work for are determined to find out who it is and why they're doing this."

This was the first time I'd heard of her working for anyone. "Who do you work for?"

She gave me a long look. "Ever heard of MI6?"

"I've seen James Bond."

"The organization I work for is a lot more secret than that." Her tone was one of finality. Clearly she wasn't going to share any more about her mysterious employers.

"So, let's go," I said. "Let's find out who's doing this."

"That's not our job, Morgan."

"I deserve the right to know why I was attacked and by whom."

She gritted her teeth. "I'm afraid that isn't possible. You need to finish your training. I told you, we've got people on it."

Fury poured through me, but I tamped it down. Maybe she could let it go that easily, but not me. I was the one who'd been attacked. Who'd *died*. I was going to hunt down the person responsible whether Kabita liked it or not.

Chapter 7

I literally had no idea what I was doing. I knew nothing about this insane world I'd suddenly been thrown into. How did one hunt down vampires who were attacking people with the hunter gene or whatever it was called?

The minute we'd finished training for the day and Kabita had gone to shower, I'd taken off. I was determined to find out what was going on.

I stomped down the street, jaw thrust forward. I'd figure it out somehow. What I wouldn't do was go back to Kabita's Fortress of friggin' Solitude. I was tired of being cooped up there. I could always stay with Clara for a bit.

That was it. Clara. The woman was an incurable gossip. She knew, like, everyone in London. She'd no doubt heard of the attacks, and she'd probably have some juicy tidbits to share. Plus she was always game for an adventure. Maybe she'd hang out with me tonight, help me find some answers. Of course, I had to be careful how I broached the subject. No way was I telling her I was a supernatural hunter on the trail of vampires. She'd laugh her ass off.

It was early yet, and I knew Clara would still be at work, so I made my way through Mayfair to a small coffee shop tucked between Clara's office building and a tapas restaurant, just behind Selfridges, the massive department store that dominated Oxford Street. I bought a caramel latte and perched on a stool in the window to wait and watch. While I sipped my hot drink, I mulled over the attacks Kabita had mentioned, trying to remember what I knew.

Not much, that was for sure. I recalled hearing a scream in an alleyway and then Kabita appearing. That must have been one of the attacks. Unfortunately, I hadn't seen anything useful. Then there'd been that news story plastered on the telly at work, the one Ana had claimed was a vampire attack. Boy, she'd freak out if she knew the truth.

And then there was the demon on the Tube. Unless I'd hallucinated that? Although I was starting to realize I hadn't. Did the demon have anything to do with the attacks, or was it a coincidence? I rubbed my forehead. At this rate, I'd be spinning my wheels, getting nowhere fast.

As darkness fell, I shivered. They'd be out now, the vamps. Hunting again, no doubt. Murdering some poor innocent. Ugh.

I tossed back the last of my latte and stepped out into the chilly night. It was nearly five, and Clara would be getting off soon. I made my way to the entrance of her building and stepped into the small lobby. It was warm inside, a little too warm, and I quickly unbuttoned my coat. There was a wooden bench against the back wall with a desk across from it. The night security guard looked up from his paper.

I gave him a wry grin as I sank down on the bench. "Waiting for someone."

He nodded, the overhead lights bouncing off his shiny scalp, and went back to his paper. The financial section. Darn. If it had been the news section, I could have snuck a look. Maybe there'd be something on the attacks.

I didn't have to wait long. Clara came sashaying out of the lift, wearing a faux fur coat in pale pink, a matching hat sitting rakishly on her dark hair.

"Girl, what are you doing here? You should have told me you were coming. Everyone, come meet my friend, Morgan. She's American." Her voice echoed against the marble walls of the lobby. Half a dozen dark eyes stared at me from under winter caps as three of Clara's co-workers gathered around to be introduced.

They were a cheerful lot, smiling and carefree. Probably had no idea there were vampires roaming the streets, waiting to suck their blood. I repressed a shiver.

"So, what are you up to? You want to come with us to dinner?" Clara asked.

"Uh, sure. I could eat."

"Good. Come along." She grabbed my arm and dragged me from the building, her friends hot on our heels.

Dinner was at an Italian joint well known for its pizza. Real pizza, like they make in Italy, not that thick crust, chemical-crammed crap they call pizza in the States.

Throughout the dinner I felt oddly uncomfortable. Clara's friends buzzed and chattered, but I was I found it difficult to focus on what they were saying. My mind was elsewhere.

"What's the matter girl?" Clara asked. "You look a million miles away."

I shrugged. "It's nothing," I said, wishing that were so. "Just my new job is hard, you know. My boss is kind of—"

"A bitch?" Clara laughed. "Aren't they all? I mean that is a boss's job. They're not happy unless they're making us miserable."

I laughed. "True that. But this is different. She wants me to be something I'm not. Even worse, she wants me to ignore the truth."

Clara gave me a funny look. "What you mean by that?"

Damn. How to explain? "Oh, you know, she wants me to ignore what's really going on. She just wants me to focus on my job like nothing else is important."

Clara frowned. "Sounds normal to me."

I knew I wasn't explaining it well, but how could I tell Clara the truth without telling her vampires were real? That monsters really did roam the night? She'd think I'd lost my mind. Heck, I thought I'd lost my mind.

Clara's colleagues started talking about going to some dance club. I didn't want to go to dance club. I had things to do. I had only one idea, and that was to roam the dark streets of London until I found a vampire and then I'd... well, I didn't know what I'd do, but I'd figure it out. It was crazy, but it was all I had. If they really were after hunters, then I had to be the perfect bait. It was my only option since Kabita couldn't help me. She seemed bound and determined to ignore what was going on. This was my life. I needed to know the truth.

"You going dancing?" Clara asked as we got up and put our coats on. Sometimes we went dancing on

Tuesday nights at the local samba place.

"Nah. Not tonight."

"Why? You got a better offer?" She laughed.

"Maybe." I lowered my voice so the others wouldn't hear. "I, um, need to meet someone."

Clara raised one eyebrow. "Someone? What someone?"

I scrambled for a believable lie. "You know how my purse went missing at the hospital? I found out who took it, and I want to confront him."

Clara's eyes grew round. "Are you kidding me? Why would you want to do that? Call the police. Let them deal with it."

"I can't prove it," I told her. "It would be my word against his. I need to find him, get him to admit the truth to me."

"Girl, you are crazy." She tied the belt of her coat around her waist. "So what's the plan?"

I shook my head. "You can't come with me. It's too dangerous."

"Which is exactly why I'm coming with you," she said stubbornly. "Now lead the way."

# # #

"Are you sure about this?" Clara murmured as the two of us huddled behind a statue in St. James Park. Through the trees I could see the floodlights surrounding the palace. I wondered vaguely if the queen was in residence and what she would think if she knew vampires roamed the streets of her city. I doubted she would be amused.

"Listen, it's the only way I can think to draw out the— ah—guy who took my stuff." I hadn't mentioned what I was really waiting for was vampires. "Once they, he, gets here, I'll confront him. Get him to admit he's guilty."

Clara looked doubtful. "How will you even find this guy?"

I couldn't exactly explain that the "he" was a vampire who had supernatural means of detection, and all I needed to do was wait. "Um, social media. He checked in a while ago. He'll have to pass by here at some point."

She frowned. "But how can you be sure? He could leave the park another way. Or what if he won't admit anything?"

I was starting to think letting Clara come along was a mistake. She asked far too many logical questions. I should have stopped her. Not that I could have. Clara was a force of nature. "I've got to at least try."

She shrugged. "Your funeral."

I winced. She had no idea how close she was. "Exactly."

"What do you want me to do?"

"Just hide out here and keep watch with me. If he does show up, hide."

"Let you approach him on your own?" She seemed aghast by the idea. "That's insane. I told you, I'm coming with you."

"No you're not. This guy is dangerous, Clara."

"Exactly," she said stubbornly. "Which is why I'm not letting you do this alone."

I sighed. This was not going according to plan. "Clara, I don't want to put you in danger." I searched wildly for a solution. "You know what would help? If we get proof this guy is the thief. You hide behind this statue and video the whole thing. Then there's no way he can deny it." The last thing I needed was a video of me plying my hunter skills against a vampire. If this got out, Kabita would go ballistic. Still, if it would keep Clara quiet and out of the way, I'd have to risk it for her sake.

She sighed as if disappointed. "If you're sure."

"I am. Trust me, this will help a lot."

I walked slowly away from our hiding place, making

sure I was clearly visible in the warm, golden glow of the park lamp nearby. Even if I could whistle, I doubt I'd have been able to. My mouth was dry as dust. I could barely swallow around the massive lump that had taken up residence in my throat. *What the hell are you thinking, Morgan?*

I wasn't. That was the problem. I just knew I needed to do *something*. A sensation hit me out of the blue. Like someone gripping the back of my skull in a tight grip. Someone very strong and not terribly nice. I winced and slapped my hand against the spot as if I could rid myself of the feeling.

"Well, if it isn't a baby hunter. Hello, Baby Hunter. Come to play with me?" The voice was a sibilant hiss in the darkness.

I froze. Bile rose, but I managed to swallow it with a wince. "Who's there? Show yourself." I tried to sound bossy and commanding like Kabita always did, but it came out far whimpier than intended.

The laugh that followed was chilling. A shadow moved at the edge of the lamplight, and I squinted, trying to make it out. Definitely humanoid, but I had a really bad feeling it wasn't human at all.

Sure enough, as he—it was definitely a male—stepped

into the light, something flashed: fangs. His eyes were infinite pools of black. Evil. I shuddered.

"Ah, I see you are afraid of me, Baby Hunter. You should be. Oh, yes, you should be."

Was Clara still hiding behind the statue, filming this? Or had she run like hell at the first sign of trouble? Gods, I hoped it was the later. If she got hurt... I shoved the thought aside. I needed to focus.

"Where are your weapons, Hunter?" I must have looked blank, because his cackle grew wilder, more excited. "No weapons? You parade about unarmed?" He leered at me. "Either you are very clever or very stupid."

I wished the answer was clever, but I really hadn't thought this far ahead. I swallowed hard. "One of you attacked me the other night," I blurted. "I want to know who it was and why."

He snorted. "Don't be ridiculous. It's not like we all talk down at the pub on a Saturday night." He circled around to the left, slowly, with purpose.

"But you know about the series of attacks." I was guessing, but I got it right.

"I've heard rumors."

"I want to know who's behind them."

He grinned wickedly, flashing fang. "Good luck with

that."

Before I could open my mouth, he had crossed the space between us and slammed me to the ground so hard, my breath wooshed from my lungs. Stars danced before my eyes as I lay, mouth opening and closing like a fish. I couldn't catch my breath. *I'm going to die.*

Shéa MacLeod

Chapter 8

"Time to die, Baby Hunter." The vamp pounced, landing on top me, knees braced on either side. He bared his fangs as he lunged for my throat. I felt the sharp scrape of teeth against delicate skin, and then there was nothing above me but empty air. I struggled up onto my elbows in time to see the vampire flying through the air. He hit the nearest lamppost with a crunch before sliding like a rag doll to the ground.

I lay there, staring at the vampire's motionless body, stunned. My breathing had returned to normal more or less, but I was still in a state of shock. I tried to scramble to my feet, but my feet weren't listening. Instead I clawed uselessly at the grass and dirt.

A figure rushed by me, headed toward the vamp. Something glinted in the dim light. It looked like a very large knife as it flashed in the figure's hand. The kind of knife that meant business.

Next thing I knew, the vamp's head was rolling across the lawn until it came to a halt a few feet away, lifeless eyes staring at me. I opened my mouth to scream, but nothing came out except an embarrassing squeak. Then it, and the vamp's body, poofed into so much dust.

I stared at the little pile of dust for a moment, then turned my attention to the newcomer. Were they dangerous? I could have smacked myself in the face. Of course the person was dangerous. They'd just beheaded a freaking vampire, for fuck's sake. Question was, were they dangerous to me?

I blinked, trying to bring the figure into focus as it hovered in the darkness just outside the light cast by the streetlamp. Based on size alone, I was guessing male. He calmly crouched, wiped the blade of the knife against the grass to clean it, then stood up, knife still in hand. My sudden relief at being rescued changed to fear. Would he behead me next? It sounded dreadfully unpleasant. I swallowed hard.

He laughed—it was definitely a he—a rusty sort of laugh that spilled up from his gut and out his throat until his whole body shook with it. I frowned. I had a bad feeling he was laughing at me.

"No need to worry, Hunter. I'm not here for you." His accent wasn't English. Scottish, maybe? But softened, like he'd lived in London a long time, and it had taken the edge off his burr.

"Well," I said tartly. "That's a relief."

He stepped into the light, and my eyes widened. He was tall, well over six feet, and rippling with muscle. I wasn't usually into shaved heads, but he carried it off in all kinds of sexy ways. His nose was a bit aquiline, but it suited him. All in all he was one sexy son of a bitch, and he knew it.

"Who are you?" I blurted.

"Connor. Connor MacRae." He stepped closer and held out his hand to help me up. I took it somewhat hesitantly. "And you are?"

"Morgan Bailey."

"What's a young hunter like you doing out without any weapons? Surely you haven't finished your training yet."

How did he even know that? "I just... um..."

He waved a hand. "Never mind. I don't want to know."

I suddenly remembered Clara. "My friend. Where is she?" I glanced around but couldn't see her.

"If you mean the woman behind the statue, taking a video, she's currently in dreamland."

"What the—" I took off running. Sure enough, Clara lay slumped on the ground, unconscious, phone still clutched in one hand. "What the hell, man? What did you do to her?"

He calmly bent down and took the phone from her and began swiping through it.

"What are you doing?" My voice was getting a bit shrill.

"I'm deleting the video," he said calmly. "Can't have that getting out. Can you imagine the panic it would cause?"

I snorted. "Nobody would believe it anyway. They'd think it was faked. Now what did you do to Clara?" I knelt down to check her pulse. I was no expert, but it seemed normal.

"I knocked her out for a bit, that's all. Jab to the nerves," he indicated with a gesture, "and down she goes. She won't remember a thing."

"Seriously. You just go around knocking people out?"

"When necessary. It's something you'll learn eventually. Can't have civilians mucking things up, getting in the way. She could have been hurt, you know." His tone was full of censure. It irked me, but I knew he was right. If Clara had gotten hurt I'd have never forgiven myself. What had I been thinking, letting her come along? Not that I'd had much choice. The woman was a force of nature.

"Hey, no sense berating yourself," he said. "You're still

new at this. Shit happens. You'll get better."

I sure hoped so. I glanced down at my sleeping friend. "How much will she remember?"

"You dragged her to the park, she was waiting, then lights out. Not much at all. I'm sure you can come up with a good cover story." He smirked.

"Sure," I said dryly. "Piece of cake."

"Come on," Connor said with a grin. "Let me take the two of you home. Least I can do."

He had saved me, yet he was offering to take us home as if he owed us? That was nice of him. Still... "I'm sorry," I said stiffly, stepping away slightly. "I don't know you."

"Hey, I get it. Tell you what." He pulled out his wallet and handed me a wad of pound notes. "You get a cab home this time. Next time you see Kabita, ask her about me."

"How do you know Kabita?"

He winked and disappeared into the dark.

#

"You did *what?*" Kabita wasn't screaming exactly, but she clearly wasn't pleased. Nope, she was furious, that much was clear.

"Listen," I snapped, "I have a right to know who attacked me and why. They need to pay for what they did, but all you seem to care about is making me punch sandbags over and over."

"Right," she snapped back. "It's called training. And it's important unless you want to end up dead your first patrol. You're lucky MacRae was there to save your ass."

It had been asking her about MacRae that had sent her on her rant. After Connor MacRae had left me in the park with an unconscious Clara, I'd called a cab and pretended Clara was just drunk. The driver either bought it or didn't care.

I managed to get her into her apartment and stayed with her until she woke the next morning. She remembered our chat, and the vampire appearing, but nothing else. And she didn't seem to realize he was anything other than a thug. She must have missed the fangs. I'd definitely have to get MacRae to teach me that move of his.

"I don't understand why I fainted," she'd said. "I never faint."

"Well, it happens to the best of us," I'd said lamely. "It was a stupid idea to begin with, and I'm sorry I let you come along."

"Hey, it was my decision," she'd said stubbornly. "I'm just glad you're okay."

"I am are. A policeman came by and chased the guy away. He wasn't who I was looking for anyway." I hated lying to my friend, but I didn't have a choice.

"What are you going to do?"

I'd shrugged. "I guess leave it to the police." She'd seemed to buy that and once she left for work, I'd headed back to Kabita's.

"So MacRae really is a legit vampire hunter?" I interrupted Kabita's rant.

She seemed nonplussed. "Well, yes, of course. Why?"

"How do you know him? Is there an annual Hunters' reunion or something?"

She held back a laugh. "Not exactly. Hunters aren't generally the socializing kind. But I've worked with him a couple of times on larger jobs."

"Jobs?"

She waved it off. "That's something we can discuss later. Right now..."

I all but stomped my foot. "Not later. Now. I'm tired of you putting me off. I need to know what I'm getting into here. What the end game is. You want me to train? Fine, I'll train, but I need to know why. And don't give me nonsense about hunting vampires or ignore what happened to me."

"I'm not ignoring it. There will be a time to address it. Now is not that time."

I bit out a growl.

Kabita heaved a sigh. "I promise you, when you're ready, we'll figure it all out. Until then you need to keep training."

"How long?"

She shook her head. "I don't know."

"Give me a ballpark here. One week? A month? Twenty years?"

"Months, all right? You should have been training since childhood, as I did, but we didn't know about you. At the bare minimum, to face down a single vampire, you'll need months of training. You may be stronger and faster than you were before, but you're not invincible. You lack control, finesse. If you went up against a vamp right now..." she paused. "Well, I guess I don't have to tell you what would happen. You're lucky MacRae was there to save your ass."

No, she didn't have to tell me. And I knew I'd lucked out having MacRae around, but she didn't have to rub my face in it. I didn't like waiting. I knew from watching true crime shows that the longer you waited, the colder the trail got. If we waited too long, we'd never discover the truth.

Kabita heaved a sigh. "Listen, if it makes you feel better, MacRae and I had a talk. While I train you, he's going to poke around, see if he can find out more info, okay?"

It did make me feel better, knowing someone was looking into it, but what I really wanted was to do it myself. "Fine. I guess you better speed up this training, because I'm not waiting forever."

Shéa MacLeod

Chapter 9

About a week passed before I saw MacRae again. I knew he and Kabita had been talking. Well, texting, but she wouldn't let me in on what was happening, which meant my frustration level was sky high. Still, I kept to my training routine, determined to be ready when the time came. I was going to be there to take down the assholes responsible for what had happened to me.

I was in the middle of sparring with Kabita when he strode into the gym with that long-limbed, loose stride of his. He leaned against the wall and watched as we circled the ring, smacking wooden swords against each other until my arm ached.

"Why don't you use real weapons?" he spoke up, twirling a toothpick between his fingers.

Kabita stopped but didn't let down her guard. "Because that's a good way for one of us to end up dead or worse."

I wasn't sure what was worse than dead. Dismemberment, maybe? Evisceration? My stomach turned at the thought of someone's guts spilling onto the floor of the ring. Yeah, that could definitely be worse.

"She'll never get any better if you play it safe." His tone was mocking.

This time Kabita did drop her guard, but I didn't bother taking advantage. She'd kick my ass but good.

"Listen, you schmuck," she snapped, whirling on Connor MacRae. "I'm her trainer. I will do as I see fit, got it?"

He held up his hands in surrender. "Whatever. I just stopped by to let you know I found something."

Kabita's eyes narrowed. "You couldn't text that?"

As his gaze met mine, I knew very well that Connor had come to tell Kabita in person because whatever the information was, it had to do with me. And he knew as well as I did, if he texted her the info, I'd never hear about it. For whatever reason, Connor was on my side.

"Fine," Kabita snarled, tossing her fake sword into the bucket with the rest of them and stomping from the ring. She snatched a towel off the ropes and mopped the light sheen of sweat that had popped up along her hairline. "Spill it, MacRae."

I leaned against one of the corner posts, sword dangling from one hand, eager to hear what Connor had to say. I didn't even care about the sweat tricking down my spine to disappear below my yoga pants. I was kind of getting used to sweating, actually.

It had never been my thing, sweating. Working out at all, really. I was a curvy woman, and I liked it that way. I never got the workout high other people seemed to experience. I just felt tired and gross afterward so, I didn't bother. Now I was suddenly faced with the reality that working out could save my life. It was annoying, but needs must and all that. Or as my mother would have said, "A woman has got to do what she must to survive in this world."

Sometimes my mother was annoyingly right.

"You look like you could use a cold drink," Connor said cheerfully, pushing himself off the wall. "Let's talk over a bottle." He sauntered toward the stairs that led up to Kabita's loft. How he knew she kept beer in the fridge was beyond me. Apparently these two were closer than I'd realized. Interesting.

The loft was exactly as one would expect: one giant room spread out across the top floor of what had once been a warehouse. Everything was in that one room: massive gourmet kitchen, cozy living room with big flat screen television, utilitarian office space with a great view of an alleyway. The bathroom was the only room tucked behind a closed door. The bedroom was up a flight of circular, wrought-iron stairs. There was a massive closet and another bathroom up there. I wasn't allowed up, but I'd peeked once. Could I help it if my curiosity was overwhelming?

I was staying in the "guest space," as Kabita referred to it. It was actually on the floor below in what had once been warehouse offices or perhaps small storage rooms. Several of the rooms had been turned into utilitarian bedrooms that were so claustrophobic, they reminded me of monks' cells in a monastery. They all shared a high school locker room-style bathroom at the end of the hall, complete with a huge open shower. Fortunately I was the only one staying there, so I had it to myself. Still, I felt oddly exposed in the massive, multi-head shower.

The floor also contained a small kitchenette across the hall from an equally small "gathering" room. The gathering room consisted of a beat-up couch and flickering TV that had seen better days, a small bistro table with two chairs, and a ping-pong table, of all things. I wondered if Kabita often trained groups of hunters and why I was the only one there. I had asked early on, but Kabita had dodged the question. She had a way of keeping things close to the vest, which was truly annoying.

Once ensconced in her fancy-ass kitchen with beers in front of us (I didn't bother to touch mine; beer is gross), Connor laid his cards on the table. Figuratively speaking.

"I've been canvassing the streets, questioning the usual suspects," he said, leaning his chair back on two legs. Kabita frowned but didn't say anything. "Nobody seems to know much of anything."

"Well, a fat lot of good that did," I snapped, irritated at how slowly it was all going. It was like they didn't want to find answers.

"Don't be hasty." He sounded amused. "I did find out something. The attacks around the city are definitely connected, and there's unquestionably a single entity behind them, although I haven't yet discovered the identity of this person other than the moniker "Mr. X." I don't even know yet if it *is* a person. Could be a conglomerate or whatnot. Or it could, quite literally, be a man with an X in his name. Who knows?"

"So basically all you've done is confirm what we already knew," Kabita said dryly.

"Yes. And it's an important step. We were guessing before. And we have the moniker, whatever good that may do us."

"What's next?" I asked.

He let the chair fall back to all fours as he drained the last of his beer. "Next, I'm going to track down this Mr. X. He or she has to have a headquarters somewhere and I aim to find it."

I stood up. "I'll come with you."

"You're not ready," Kabita said. Her tone was calm but final.

"Oh, come on, K," Connor said in a mocking tone, "if it were up to you, she'd never be ready. Let me take her out, show her the ropes. Get in some real-world training."

"I'm all for that," I agreed eagerly. "I'm so over this fake sword-play bullshit."

Kabita glowered at both of us. "This is not a good idea."

"Come on," Connor wheedled. "She'll be with me. I'll watch out for her. Promise." He winked at me. I wasn't sure what the joke was, but I would be glad to be out of this place and doing something real for a change.

"Fine," Kabita growled, "but if things go pear-shaped, don't say I didn't warn you."

# # #

Taking the Tube to my first official hunt wasn't exactly

what I had in mind. I was supposed to be a badass vampire hunter, for goodness sake, and there I was, sitting on blue-and-orange carpeted seats like every other rat on the wheel. How was I supposed to carry weapons on the Tube? Not that I had any. Connor was bringing those. But if I had, it would have been awkward. Not that anyone would have noticed. Ninety percent of the travelers had their noses stuck in a book, ereader, or newspaper. The other ten percent were either playing video games on their phones or totally wrapped up in whatever conversation they were having. No one even noticed me.

The car slid to a stop at London Bridge Station and half the occupants surged toward the open doors. I followed them more slowly, not in any particular rush to meet Connor. Now that it was upon me, I wasn't sure I wanted "real world" experience. What I wanted was to go back to my nice safe world with my little flat share and my boring job and my normal routine. I hadn't signed up to hunt supernatural whatsit. That wasn't the plan at all. Not that I'd had much of a plan, but it certainly wasn't this.

I stepped onto the bottom of the escalator, right hand lightly balanced on the moving rail as it swept me ever upward toward my destiny. Destiny. That was a load of crock. My destiny was to travel Europe, enjoy life. Maybe find a nice guy and settle down. This was not the destiny I wanted. Unfortunately, it appeared to be what I was stuck with.

I swiped my Oyster Card on the yellow reader, and the gate swung open to let me pass. Cold air rushed in through the wide exit ahead. People dodged left and right, rushing in and out of the station in a never-ending tide.

"Having second thoughts?"

I glanced up, startled to find Connor striding next to me. "I thought we were supposed to meet at the flower stall near the market."

He grinned. "I figured you might need some Dutch courage first," he said, handing me a silver flask. I caught a whiff of alcohol, something strong and oaky. Whisky, maybe. Or bourbon. I'm not good with these things.

"Is this a good idea? Hunting while drunk?"

That got a full belly laugh out of him. "You're not getting drunk. You're taking a nice long swallow to take the edge off. Trust me, your first hunt? You're going to want this."

With a shrug, I swallowed a mouthful of the stuff. It burned all the way down, making my eyes water and my lungs wheeze.

"Not used to the hard stuff, eh?" He took the flask from me and screwed the cap on before shoving it in his hip pocket.

"Do cocktails count?"

He snickered. "Figures."

I glared. "What's that supposed to mean?"

"Oh, here we are." He stopped in front of a row of stalls. Above the wide aisle, a sign hung. Borough Market.

"Why hunt here?" I asked. "It's closed." The market was only open until five, six on Friday, but this was a Thursday. It was nearly eight and the market had been empty for hours. Everything was dark, and shadows loomed ominously. "Why would vampires hang out here? No one to munch on."

"You'd be surprised. It's quiet so it's a good place to gather. And it's close enough to food sources they can easily grab and run."

"Ew."

He chuckled. "Exactly."

"What's the plan?"

He rolled his shoulders as if loosening the muscles. "Word has it there's a small nest that's been making itself at home here. We go in and clean it out." He pulled what looked like a claymore from a sheath on his back.

"Jesus."

He smirked. "Quite. This one's for you." He retrieved another blade from a second sheath and handed it to me.

I turned it over in my hands. It had obviously been well used. "A machete? Really?"

"Don't knock it. It's light, easy to work with, and it's a sharp motherfucker. A good hack or two with that thing, and you're going to have one headless vamp. A machete doesn't require much experience or finesse. It's a dirty blade for a dirty job. Trust me."

"Whatever," I said with some exasperation. "I just wish I got the cool sword."

"I doubt you could lift the cool sword. For now, you're better off with the machete."

"You're the boss."

He gave me a stern look. "And don't forget it. Now follow me and keep as quiet as possible."

I nodded and plunged after him into the darkness.

Chapter 10

To my right, a monster leaned out of the darkness, ready to eat me whole. I nearly jumped out of my skin until I realized it was a lopsided stack of half busted crates. I shivered and gripped the handle of my machete a little tighter.

Ahead of me, Connor moved like a ghost, feet absolutely silent against the concrete floor of the market. The ceiling soared overhead, and I imagined vamps hovering above, staring down at us with bloodthirsty eyes. I repressed a shudder as memories of my attack flooded back. I pushed them aside ruthlessly. Now was not the time.

Connor waved me forward, and I stepped to his side. We'd reached the exit of the main market hall. Beyond, the grounds stretched out, taking up space beneath the underbelly of London Bridge. I knew from past visits that the brick arches of the bridge soared even higher than the market ceiling. It would be a perfect place for a vamp nest to make its home. The noise from the bridge drowned out any other sound, making it a perfect killing ground. As long as there were no inconvenient leftovers for people to find come morning. The thought made me a little queasy.

Connor motioned to the right, around an aisle of booths. I nodded and started that way, pausing when I realized he hadn't followed. I turned, but in the inky blackness I could no longer see him. Trepidation sent my heart racing.

"Connor?" I whispered as softly as possible. There was no answer. *Where could he be? What if something had happened to him?*

Not sure what else to do, I continued around the path to the right, following orders. Surely Connor had a plan. He was the official hunter, after all. I was just the trainee.

I held the machete blade in front of me like a ward against evil. I almost laughed aloud at the silliness of it. I had my doubts as to its effectiveness in a fight against a vamp.

And then I felt it. That awful grip on the back of my skull, squeezing until a headache burst behind my eyes. I wanted to scream at it to stop, whatever it was, but if there were vamps nearby, they'd hear me.

From the darkness ahead, I heard a rustling. Was it Connor? No, couldn't be. He wouldn't have made it around the path yet

It rushed at me, roaring out of the shadows like the spawn of hell in a bad dream. There was little light to see. Its face was a pale blur, but I could make out its extended, claw-like fingers, ready to rake the skin from my face. I ducked and barely missed losing an eye.

"Connor!" I screamed, but there was no answer. The grip of the machete was slick with sweat. My palms slipped a little, and panic surged to the surface. *What the hell are you doing, you idiot?*

The animal part of me, the one that's been with us since we crawled out of the sea and into caves, urged me to run. But the part of me, the hunter part, the part Kabita had been working on for well over a month, screamed at me to stand my ground. Running would get me killed. Fight and I might live to see dawn.

I dodged as a clawed hand slashed out of the darkness, raking a bloody furrow down my bicep. It stung like a motherfucker. I hefted the machete and swung with everything I had. It wasn't a solid hit, but I must have scratched it because the vamp let out a howl. Pain or anger, I wasn't sure which, and I didn't care. Marking the spot I'd heard the scream, I lashed out again. This time the machete connected solidly, sinking deep into muscle and tissue. This time the scream nearly deafened me. I tried to pull the blade out, but whatever it was in, it was stuck fast. There was no budging it.

Shitshitshit.

Forgetting my training, I turned and ran like hell. I didn't have a choice. I'd lost my weapon and was fighting blind, and Connor? Nowhere to be found. Asshole.

I darted around a booth, ghostly white in the darkness. My feet skidded on a piece of loose stone from the pavement. The vamp hit me full in the back, and I went down hard, scraping knees and palms. Ignoring the pain, I bucked wildly, dislodging the vampire. It crashed into the nearest booth, crunching the wood to matchsticks.

Scrambling to my feet, I ran again, dashing and darting around booths, trying to lose the vampire. It was no use. The creature was gaining on me.

And then Connor was there, slashing and hacking with his massive sword. Bright light coming from somewhere in the vicinity of his head shone on the battle. The wicked blade cut deep, splattering arterial spray across the old bricks. I stumbled back, bile rising in my throat, until my back was pressed against the cold hardness of the wall behind me.

Finally he ended it. One slash and, like the first vamp Connor had killed in front of me, this one's head went rolling along the concrete until it came to a halt in front of the cheese booth, where it, and the body behind it, dusted. I didn't think I'd ever look at cheese the same way again.

Oh, who was I kidding? No amount of vampire gore would ever put me off cheese.

Connor pulled a red handkerchief from his back pocket and calmly wiped his blade clean before sheathing it. He gave me a mild look. "You okay?"

"Okay?" I screeched, suddenly furious. "You left me alone in the dark with that thing. It nearly killed me. And where did you get that light?" I asked, pointing at the biker's light strapped around his head. "Why didn't you give me one?"

He swooped down to collect my now freed machete. "You're bleeding, Morgan."

"What?" I glanced down, and sure enough, rivulets of blood slid down my arm. Suddenly it hurt like a son of a bitch. Half sting, half ache. Crap. The thing had probably given me tetanus. When was the last time I'd had shots?

"I didn't know where it was, or I would have taken this route," he said calmly, using the same handkerchief he'd used to wipe his blade to soak up the blood on my arm. That couldn't possibly be sanitary. "The light... I only had the one." He shrugged as he pulled a packet out of his breast pocket and ripped it open. The scent of rubbing alcohol stung my nose as he wiped down my cut.

"Fuck, that stings."

"Better than getting an infection," he said calmly.

By the time he'd finished, the bleeding had already stopped, scabs forming along the furrows. I was sure to have a hell of a scar.

"If you're worried about scarring, don't."

"You a mind reader now?" I said, a little more sharply than I'd meant.

He grinned. "Nope. But I've been there. Hunters don't scar. Not unless it's a magical relic. Fingernails, fangs, blades? Won't do anything but hurt for a while. Remember, we heal faster than normal."

"Yeah, yeah. I'm still pissed at you."

"I assume you mean American pissed."

I gave him a look. "Since British pissed means getting drunk, yeah."

He looped an arm casually around my shoulders. "I can deal. How about we go get British pissed. I'd say we earned it."

I was all for that, but then a thought struck. "What about the nest?"

He glanced behind him. "Intel must have been wrong. That one was the only one here. Now let's find a pub. I feel like celebrating."

# # #

"You know, Morgan," Connor slurred as we staggered toward the side door of Kabita's warehouse, "you're the prettiest hunter. And I'm not jusht shaying that. I mean it. I really do."

"Thanks, man," I said, patting him on his inebriated back. I'd only had one pint of rather warm beer, and I hadn't even finished it. I hated beer, but Connor had insisted that cider, especially pear cider, was the drink of pansies. Which I told him was stupid. They'd been out of pear cider anyway, and Connor had smirked and ordered me a beer. As for him, I'd lost count after the first three pints. I guessed he needed to celebrate, all right. "You can sleep it off in one of the spare rooms. Kabita has plenty."

I had no idea how Kabita would feel having a drunk Connor stay over, but it seemed irresponsible to let him out in public in such a state. He couldn't drive anyway; his car was parked safely in the parking lot out front, thanks to me. I figured the best bet was to have him sober up before sending him on his way. I couldn't imagine anyone having a problem with it.

I managed to get him through the door and up the short flight of stairs to the "ground" floor (what Americans would refer to as the first floor, though it was actually more like halfway between ground floor and first floor, thanks to the high ceilings in the basement). I shoved open the first door on the left, revealing a room identical to my own: narrow bed with metal frame, utilitarian nightstand with simple ceramic lamp, narrow wardrobe in cheap pine. That was it, and that was plenty. The space was so small, there was barely enough room for me to maneuver him to the bed.

I dropped him, and he landed with an *oomph* before letting out a loud snore. I shook my head, not sure whether to be annoyed or amused. I decided to play nice and strode down the hall to the kitchenette, where I filled a glass with water. Returning to Connor's room, I placed it on the bedside table, then shut the door on the room and him. It was late, and exhaustion tugged at me. My arm itched like crazy, which was weird, and the beer had made my mouth taste foul. I wanted to brush my teeth, get on my pajamas, and hit the hay. No doubt Kabita would have me up at some ungodly hour again.

I kicked off my boots and left them, and my clothes, in the middle of my bedroom floor. Yanking on a pair of pink, striped pajamas, I padded to the bathroom. I left my toiletries in the bathroom instead of keeping them in my room. Who was there to mess with them?

Squirting toothpaste on my toothbrush, I went about the business of preparing for bed. My eyes drooped. Gods, I wanted my bed so badly, even if it was one of the hardest, most uncomfortable things I'd ever slept on.

Back in my room, I was asleep before my head hit the pillow.

I have no idea what woke me. Maybe it was Connor snoring in the other room, or maybe there were rats in the walls, but whatever it was, one minute I was so deeply asleep I was literally drooling. The next I was wide awake, straining to see in the pitch blackness of my room, fingers itching for the machete Connor had loaned me earlier. I held my breath, listening for anything out of place.

There it was—a faint scrape down the hall. It wasn't Connor. He was still snoring loud enough to wake the dead.

Carefully pulling back the covers, I slipped out of bed and padded to the door. As quietly as possible, I turned the handle and opened it a mere inch or two, just enough to peek out. A light shone from the kitchen. I sniffed. Coffee. My mouth watered. It was three in the damn morning. Who was making coffee at this hour? I couldn't imagine Kabita would be down here instead of in her own kitchen.

With no other weapon at hand, I unplugged my lamp. Leaving the shade on the nightstand, I held it by the narrow head like a club. Whoever it was was going to wish they'd stayed out of this building.

I made my way silently to the kitchen and peered around the corner. My eyes widened. *Holy mother of pearl*

"Come on in," said a cheerful masculine voice. "I made coffee."

Chapter 11

He wasn't tall, maybe a couple inches shy of six feet, but he was nicely built in that lean muscled way I liked, with broad shoulders and narrow hips. His eyes were bright blue behind wire-rimmed glasses, and his tousled hair, nearly shoulder length, was golden brown or maybe dark blond. It was hard to tell under the fluorescents. What I could tell was that he was gorgeous in a geeky kind of way. He was also very young. Jesus, was he even out of high school yet?

"Who the hell are you?" Finding strange men in my kitchen at 3:00 a.m. doesn't do well for my manners. My mother would have been horrified.

"Oh, sorry." He swiped a hand against jeans-clad legs, then held it out as if expecting me to shake. "Inigo Jones."

"Jones?" I ignored the hand, which he dropped to his side.

"Yes. Kabita's cousin."

Cousin? Dammit. He was probably off limits. Not that I was interested, of course.

"She didn't tell you I was coming?"

"Er, no," I admitted. "No, she did not."

"I'm truly sorry about that. Coffee?" He held up the glass pot. I'd insisted we have a proper drip pot. I was done with instant. I didn't know how anyone could drink that stuff.

"Um, sure. I guess."

"Brilliant." He busied himself, pouring a cup for each of us. His accent was British but faint, as if he'd lived elsewhere for a long time and had mostly assimilated.

"Where did you come from exactly?" I asked as he handed me an avocado green mug that looked like it was left over from the '70s. Probably it was.

"America," he side with a wide grin that was too sexy for comfort. "Your neck of the woods."

"How do you know what neck of the woods I'm from?"

"Kabita told me you're from Portland. The Oregon one, of course." Teeth flashed again. "I recently took up residence in that fair city after six years in Seattle."

Which explained the accent or near lack of one. "I see. And you came for a visit."

"Indeed. Got in this morning, but I had errands and such. I didn't mean to wake you. My system is a little wonky at the moment."

I got it. It had taken me some time to adjust from Pacific to Greenwich Mean Time. There had been many restless nights and drowsy mornings the first couple of weeks after I'd arrived in London. "No problem. Just, uh, freaked me out a bit."

"Yeah, sorry about that."

I shrugged, not sure what else to say. "I guess you know about this place then."

"Kabita's stronghold? Rather. And her training ground, definitely. I've been known to help with training from time to time, although I'm really rather more of a tech guy. Gadgets, IT, that sort of thing."

"Oh. Interesting," I said lamely. "Are you a hunter, too?"

He snorted. "Not at all. Normal old human, I'm afraid. Kabita says your training is going well, more or less."

I winced. "Yeah. I'm kind of over it. I don't know what she expects, but beating the shit out of sandbags every day is getting old."

He grinned. "Kabita does tend to be stuck in her ways." He sobered. "I hear you met Connor MacRae."

"Yep. He took me on a real hunt. It was pretty exciting." I left out the part about him nearly getting me eaten. I didn't want *that* getting back to Kabita. She'd never let me out of the fortress again. "In fact, he got a little wasted celebrating afterward, so he's sleeping it off in one of the guest rooms."

"That explains the ungodly snoring."

It was my turn to apologize. "Uh, sorry. I had no idea anyone else was staying here. And I had no idea he snored."

He waved it off. "Not like I'm sleeping anyway." He held up the pot. "More coffee?"

"No. This was plenty. Thanks." I walked over to the sink to rinse out my mug. I caught a whiff of chocolate and something smoky, like campfires and roasted marshmallows. Maybe it was his shampoo or something.

Setting the mug next to the coffee maker to reuse in the morning, I turned to smile at Inigo. He was watching me intently with an odd expression on his face. I wasn't sure what to make of it, so I ignored it.

"It was nice meeting you," I said. "Guess I'll see you in the morning. Night."

"Goodnight, Ms. Bailey. Sleep well."

Frankly, I wasn't sure I'd sleep at all.

# # #

"I've got it!"

I glanced up, startled, from my orange juice and peanut butter toast to see Connor come striding into the gathering room, waving his cellphone in the air. He plopped into the chair opposite me and grabbed the juice pitcher.

"Got what?"

He splashed a bit of juice into a glass, tossed it back, and then grinned at me. "I know where Mr. X is."

"The person behind the attacks? Where? How?"

He leaned forward and braced his arms on the table. I suddenly realized he was shirtless, and it became him exceedingly well. "Prague."

I frowned. "Why on earth is someone in Prague doing ordering attacks on people in London?"

Connor leaned back, expression pensive. "Well, that's another story and one I don't have the answer to, unfortunately. However, I have it on good authority that Mr. X is definitely in Prague." He tapped his phone. "One of my CIs texted me this morning."

"You have confidential informants?" I asked around a mouthful of toast.

"Of course. Any good hunter does. Like the police and whatnot."

"And one of these informants says Mr. X is in Prague." I frowned. "Don't you find that a bit weird?"

"Honey, I deal in weird. This whole supernatural hunter thing is weird. Believe me, you get used to it."

"Are you going?" I asked.

"Of course."

"Then I want to go with you."

"Go where?" Kabita strode into the room, boots thumping on the wood plank floor.

"I'm going to Prague with Connor. He's found Mr. X."

Kabita's face looked like a thundercloud. "Oh no, you are not."

"Excuse me," I said angrily, "but you can't stop me. I have every right to be there when he brings down the person responsible for the attack on me. Besides, I can help."

She snorted with laugher. "Are you serious? You nearly got yourself killed last night."

My jaw dropped. "How do you know about that?" I glared at Connor, who held up his hands.

"I didn't tell her."

"I'm not an idiot," Kabita snapped. "I have no doubt about what happened last night. Connor left you on your own, and you nearly got your ass handed to you."

She was a little too close to the money for my comfort. What I wanted to know was how she knew what had happened. I hadn't told her, and I'd bet my bottom dollar, Connor hadn't said anything. Since no one but the dead vamp had been there to witness the event, that left one explanation: Connor had a reputation. Or Kabita had an opinion of him, earned or not. But whatever the reason, Kabita expected this behavior of him, which didn't bode well for any future real life training.

"She handled herself quite well," Connor said, unperturbed by Kabita's accusations. "I guarantee she learned more last night than she has in the entire month you've had her playing with wooden sticks."

He had a point. As scared and irked I'd been, I'd learned quite a lot. And while he'd had to save me—again—I'd gotten in a few good whacks. I now knew what it was to face down a vampire armed only with a blade and a meager amount of practice. Likely I'd have died if Connor hadn't come to my rescue, but next time I'd know more. I'd do better.

"He's got a point." Logic came from an unexpected source. Inigo had sauntered in and was leaning against the counter, coffee mug in hand, looking just as delicious as he had last night. "You can't keep her locked up in your ivory tower forever. At some point you've got to let her out into the real world."

"You stay out of this," Kabita snapped. "I'm the trainer."

"As I was telling Morgan and Kabita," Connor interjected, turning to Inigo, "I've had more info from my CI. Looks like our Mr. X is in Prague."

"And I'm going with him," I said firmly.

"You're not going. You're staying here to finish your training," Kabita said.

"Don't I have a say in this?" I practically shouted in frustration. "This person tried to have me killed, after all. This is personal."

"And that's the problem," she snapped, "You're letting emotion get in the way. Plus, you aren't even close to finishing your training. Heading to a foreign country to hunt vampires in an unfamiliar city is stupid, reckless, and dangerous."

"I'd be with her," Connor said.

Kabita snorted. "Look how well that turned out. No. Absolutely not. Now come on. Time to start training for the day."

As I got up to follow her, annoyed by her refusal but

unsure what to do about it. Connor caught my eye and winked. I repressed a grin and winked back. I guess I was going to Prague after all, whether Kabita agreed with the plan or not.

Shéa MacLeod

Chapter 12

"Wow! This is amazing. I can't believe this place is real." I stared about me in wonder, my senses on overload.

Prague was like a fairy tale. The air was perfumed with cinnamon and sugar from the *trdelnik*, cinnamon- and sugar-covered pastries wrapped around a cylinder and baked over an open fire. It seemed every other shop offered it, luring in the tourists with the promise of a sugar rush they'd never forget.

A multitude of languages assaulted my ears, and tourists and locals alike strolled along the narrow roads. Street musicians joined in the cacophony with cheerful tunes on guitars, violins, and accordions.

Fantastical buildings painted in ice cream colors, and studded with elaborate bas relief, stood against the bright blue sky. The streets were paved in ancient gray cobblestones, and on the hill above the city loomed the palace complex, elegant and mysterious, with the cathedral spire rising above it. Wonder of wonders, our hotel was built into the wall of the palace itself, halfway down the hill, or up, depending on your viewpoint, the winding street outside it picture perfect.

"Come on," Connor urged. "I know a great place for goulash with bread dumplings. Trust me, you're going to love it."

"Shouldn't we be hunting Mr. X?"

"We will," he assured me, "but we need sustenance first. It's just up there." He pointed toward a red-fronted building with a golden lion painted on a sign swinging out front. A friendly middle-aged woman dressed in white-and-black greeted us with a big smile and heavily accented English, ushered us inside, and seated us at a cozy table in a corner away from the chilly air of the open door.

The waitress beamed at us and moved a candle to our table. "More romantic," she said.

I opened my mouth to tell her Connor and I weren't a couple, but she was already gone. "Well, that was awkward," I muttered.

Connor laughed. "Don't worry about it. Who cares what anyone thinks? Besides, the candlelight is nice."

We both ordered the beef goulash, which came on large plates with steamed bread dumplings. The savory fragrance of the rich sauce tickled my nose, and my stomach let out an unladylike growl, which Connor politely ignored. We dug in with gusto. The beef was melt-in-your-mouth tender, the sauce rich and meaty, and the dumplings bland but a perfect setting for the goulash. Connor had even ordered a red wine that perfectly complemented the meal.

"Would you like dessert?" the waitress asked as she collected our dirty plates. "Apple strudel with homemade vanilla ice cream is our specialty."

"When in Rome, eh?" Connor asked with a wink. I was all for that.

After the waitress left, Connor excused himself to use the men's room. I sat enjoying the candle-lit ambiance and the classical music playing over the stereo system. There were only two other couples in the restaurant, as it was still quite early for dinner.

Time passed, and I grew restless. Connor had been gone longer than I expected. The waitress arrived with steaming apple strudels, the vanilla ice cream already melting in rich puddles.

"Hope it doesn't get cold before he gets back," I mused.

"Oh, I'm sure he'll be in soon."

I frowned. "In?" Maybe her English was rough and she meant "out." He'd only gone to the bathroom.

She nodded toward the open front door. "He is talking

to his friend. Didn't you know? I'm sure he won't be long. I will go out and tell him dessert is come." She smiled and hurried across the floor.

Through the open restaurant door, I saw Connor talking to a strange man. The man looked a little on the rough side with his beat-up leather jacket and European-style jeans worn at the knees. His face was craggy and weather-beaten, and his eyes darted around constantly, as if he was looking for something. Definitely not a tourist. Maybe one of Connor's CIs?

I decided not to wait and dug into the sweet spiciness of the strudel. I kept one eye on the door, waiting for Connor to return. I was nearly done with my dessert by the time he did.

"What was that about?" I asked before he'd hardly sat down.

"What?" He gave me a blank look, but I wasn't buying it.

"That man you were talking to."

"Oh, him. Just some beggar asking for money." He shrugged it off.

The conversation had been a lot longer than just a quest for spare change. A lot more intense, too. Still, I figured the guy was probably a CI, and Connor was hiding his identity. I decided to let it go. Wasn't my business.

"This strudel is amazing," Connor said, swapping the subject. "I wonder if they'll let me have seconds."

"I imagine they will as long as you pay for it," I said. "Let's talk about Mr. X."

"Not here. Too many ears. Later." He waved over the waitress. "I'm definitely getting a second strudel."

# # #

It had rained while we were in the restaurant, and the dark street, lit by the soft glow of antique-style streetlamps, shone glossy. It was like looking at a postcard. The street swept down the hill and curved slightly to the left, lined with gorgeous old stone buildings, mysterious in the darkness. I was feeling mellow and chill, my belly full of delicious food and wine.

We were nearly to the hotel when one shadow separated itself from the rest. The light glinted off something far more sinister than wet cobblestones. A knife flashed in the figure's hand, and I froze. I was unarmed. Hopefully Connor had a weapon, or we were screwed.

I recognized the craggy-faced man from the restaurant, the one Connor had been talking to. Surely a CI wouldn't attack his... whatever it was Connor was. Handler? I turned to glance at the hunter, but he was nowhere to be seen.

Fuck. Where the hell was he? He'd been beside me just a moment ago. Suddenly it didn't matter because the dude was coming at me, brandishing that knife like he meant to use it.

Craggy Face rushed me, snarling like an animal. Shit, vamps were ugly in Prague. I dodged to the right, narrowly missing his blade but slamming my shoulder into the wall of the nearest building in the process. I winced a little at the impact.

He tried again, and this time I lashed out with one booted foot. I put everything I had into it, catching him in the knee with a sickening crunch. I stared, surprised, as he went down, howling in pain. His leg had snapped like a proverbial twig.

"You're not a vampire," I blurted.

He stared at me like I was crazy and muttered something incomprehensible. I was pretty sure it involved something anatomically impossible.

I stepped toward him, and he blanched. Holding out a

hand, he babbled something definitely not in English—I could only assume it was Czech—before using a parked car to haul himself to his feet. Then he limped off in haste. How, I had no idea. I was pretty sure I'd done some serious, permanent damage.

I felt a little guilty. I wasn't supposed to hurt humans. But the dude had been intent on slicing my throat, so what could a girl do?

"Oh, there you are."

I spun around to find Connor sauntering toward me like he hadn't a care in the world. "Where the hell have you been?" I snapped, angry he'd left me alone to face Craggy Face alone. Sure I was technically a hunter, but I was mostly untrained. Connor was supposed to be training me, not leaving me in dangerous situations by myself.

He gave me a baffled look. "Forgot my wallet. Went back to get it."

"And you didn't say anything?"

"Of course I did. I guess you didn't hear me."

Suddenly I doubted myself. I had been so busy admiring the scenery, maybe I hadn't heard him. "Next time talk louder."

"What's gotten into you?"

"Some dude attacked me."

"What?" He looked suitably horrified. "What happened?"

"That guy you were talking to at the restaurant? The one you said asked you for money? He came after me. With a knife."

Connor's eyes widened. "Did he hurt you?"

"No. I thought he was a vamp, so I kicked him in the leg with full hunter strength."

Connor winced.

"Exactly. Probably will never be the same. Maybe he'll think twice before attacking innocent tourists." I eyed Connor. "Why would he attack me anyway?"

He sighed. "It's my fault. I should have known this would happen. It's not unheard of for a criminal to pretend to beg for money, then later mug the person. I'm guessing that was his plan."

It made sense, but something niggled at me. Something that made me uneasy. I just wasn't sure what it was.

Chapter 13

The sun shone bright on the St. Charles Bridge stretching across the Vltava River. On either side of it, carved stone statues of saints, turned black with age, stood as silent sentinels to the proceedings below. Artisans of every imaginable variety had set up carts and booths, selling everything from photographs of the bridge to wood-carved trinkets, snaring tourists with claims of great deals. Beggars knelt on the bridge, foreheads pressed to the cobblestones. Empty hats sat before them, waiting to be filled. Some hats had a few coins, others nothing. I felt sorry for the beggars. They seemed a sorry lot.

Connor ignored the unfortunate souls, whistling as he walked along with his loose-limbed stride. It didn't escape me that many women glanced his way with appreciative smiles and speculative expressions. He was, after all, a very attractive man, though perhaps not a terribly attentive or kind one. Maybe it was a hunter thing? Kabita wasn't exactly soft-hearted.

The bridge led us into the town center, where we passed beneath the formidable bridge tower and into the old town. Tourists flooded the streets, jostling us from every side. I found it annoying and applied elbows with frequent abandon, but Connor seemed unmoved, totally intent on our destination.

We headed down a street that seemed far too narrow to allow for cars. On either side pressed various shops: bakeries, souvenirs, and Thai massage parlors. Above one of the massage places, a flag waved from an open window. I caught a figure peering out and stumbled to a stop with surprise. Yep. I hadn't been mistaken. It was Predator, from the movie. Predator was standing in the open window of a Thai massage parlor, waving a flag. I shook my head, amused.

Connor led me farther down the street to a second massage parlor, one minus the Predator. We passed through a wide doorway into a room furnished with what looked more or less like lawn chairs. Each had a bright green cushion. Several of them contained fully dressed clients, mostly tourists, getting massages from tiny Thai women. The massages seemed to involve a lot of stretching, pounding, and painful looking kneading. I was slightly embarrassed at the image "Thai massage parlor" had stirred up. These places were relaxing, Zen, and perfectly respectable.

Connor stopped at the front desk, where an older Thai woman sat knitting, orange reading glasses perched on her nose. He spoke to her in Czech, and she quickly answered. I'd had no idea Connor spoke the language. The man was full of surprises.

"Upstairs," he said in English.

I nodded and followed him to the back of the room, where a wide set of stone steps led upward to the first floor. Our boots thumped on stone as we trudged up in the dim light. Small windows let in a meager amount of sunlight, barely illuminating the way. At the top of the steps was an ancient wooden door bound in brass and intricately carved. A scarlet cord hung to one side, and Connor gave it a firm tug. I heard the faint jangle of a bell from the other side of the door.

It seemed like twenty minutes passed, though it was probably more like two or three, before the heavy door ponderously swung open. On the other side stood a large Asian man with a pot belly and a massive mustache, which drooped over his lips. I wondered how he ate without getting hair in his mouth.

"We're here to see Bosko," Connor said, his expression stoic and his tone firm. I noticed he'd puffed up his chest a bit, as if to appear larger. I barely managed to hold back an eye roll at the posturing.

"Come." The Asian man stood aside to allow us to pass through before slamming the door so hard, it echoed through the large hall. The ceiling soared nearly fifteen feet high, braced with thick oak beams that looked as if they'd been there hundreds of years. The walls were the same stone as the steps and bare of any decor. The long hall was lined with several doors of normal size and recent age, interspersed with sconces that, while electric, looked medieval. What on earth was this place? Was this the brothel I'd expected downstairs?

"Wait," the large man snapped before spinning on his heel and striding down the hall. He paused before one of the doors, glanced back to make sure we'd remained in place, opened the door, and slipped inside.

"What is going on?" I whispered to Connor. All he'd told me earlier was that we were going to meet a "contact" who had information on our Mr. X. He'd refused to answer any further questions, which had been more than a little annoying.

Connor indicated I should be quiet, which irritated me beyond belief. I wanted answers. I wanted to know what the hell this place was and why we were here. But what if there were secret cameras or something? Maybe Connor was afraid someone was eavesdropping, and this was a top secret meeting. I remained silent.

It was definitely more than twenty minutes before the large man returned. My back was aching from standing still so long, and I desperately wanted to sit down. I kept shifting from one foot to the other, trying to get comfortable, until Connor glared at me. I ignored him. It wasn't his back that was hurting.

Finally the door swung open, and Mr. Mustache waved at us to join him. Without a word, Connor tromped down the hall with me hot on his heels. Mustache waved us inside and slammed the door, nearly hitting me in the butt. I heared his footsteps retreating back to the entrance. I wished he'd have stayed long enough I could give him a dirty look.

The room was small, about eight foot by eight foot. The size of a child's bedroom. Swaths of red, green, and gold silk hung from the beams to form elegant folds and drapes. Sunlight through a small window decorated with stained glass sent colorful prisms dancing across the wood floor. Simple glass-and-brass lanterns flickered with ambient light, and the room smelled strongly of incense, something musky that tickled my nose. Against the wall in front of us was a low platform on which sat a thin mattress. On the mattress lay an equally thin man, clothed in what looked like silk pajamas. A Thai woman was currently walking on his back. I wasn't sure if it looked good or painful.

The man turned his head, propping his left cheek on his forearm so he could see Connor and me. He had wispy, blond hair and blue eyes set off by the pale blue of his pajamas. He looked to be about thirty, a few years older than me. "MacRae. What a pleasure." His accent was definitely Czech, and his tone made it clear seeing Connor was anything but pleasurable.

"It's been a long time, Bosko." Connor's tone was easygoing, but there was a grimness to his eyes.

"Too long," Bosko said, waving off the Thai woman and sitting up. He smoothed his thin hair, clearly trying to cover the bald spots while trying not to look like he cared about such things.

Connor grunted, noncommittal.

"To what do I owe this visit?" Bosko asked, standing slowly. Next to Connor he looked positively reedy, but there was something about him that felt dangerous, even in bare feet and pajamas.

"I need some intel."

Bosko smirked. "So you thought of me. How

flattering."

"You know you're the best."

Bosko inspected the nails of his left hand. "Naturally. You know it will cost you."

"Naturally," Connor echoed Bosko's word dryly.

"What is it you need?" He sank elegantly back onto the cushions at one end of the mattress and waved at us to do the same. Since there was nowhere to sit but the floor, we both sat cross-legged. It wasn't terribly comfortable.

"Mr. X."

Bosko's pale eyebrows nearly hit his receding hairline. "Pardon?"

"I have intel there is an entity in Prague referring to himself or herself, as Mr. X. Mr. X is responsible for several vampire attacks in London. The victims were all potential hunters."

This time Bosko seemed genuinely interested. "And you want me to find out about this Mr. X and his, dastardly plan?"

"If you would be so kind." Connor's voice dripped sarcasm.

"No need to be so prickly, dear boy. I just might have what you're looking for." He raised his arms so the sleeves of his pajamas fell back, revealing skinny, pale arms. He clapped twice, sharp and loud. The door swung open, and the same Thai girl who'd been on his back popped her head in. "Naak, bring my laptop, please."

Naak bowed her head, her glossy black hair swinging forward, then turned and disappeared. A moment later she returned, computer in hand. She handed it to Bosko and left, shutting the door behind her. The minute she was gone, Bosko flipped open the laptop and began tapping away on the keys.

"About a month ago, I began to notice an interesting shift in the power of the old town."

I blinked, confused. The power of the old town? What did that mean? Before I could open my mouth to ask, Bosko smiled at me.

"I see you are not familiar with my fair city. Let me explain. For centuries, the city of Prague has been guarded against many supernatural evils by the gargoyles."

"Gargoyles? Prague has honest-to-gods gargoyles?" I'd seen them, of course. They were everywhere. But I'd assumed they were simple stone carvings, as they were in London, Paris, and most other places. True gargoyles were a rare creature.

Bosko beamed. "Indeed."

"Do we really need to go through this?" Connor snarled. I was annoyed and surprised by his sudden rudeness.

"Knowledge is power, dear boy. Besides, I like storytelling. Where was I? Yes, the gargoyles have considered Prague their own and have guarded us for centuries, but a month ago, things changed. Gargoyles stopped shifting, remaining frozen in stone, unable to attend their duties. There are only two hunters in the city, as there is little for them to do, but one disappeared and the other ended up dead. Tourists have gone missing. Bodies are found in the river in surprising numbers, and more and more strange creatures have begun appearing where they should not be." His expression had taken on a grim cast. Clearly Bosko was not thrilled by the changing events.

"You're only pissed because losing control over the supernatural means losing power yourself," Connor said.

"Perhaps, but something had gone amiss, and I was determined to discover what was happening. One name kept popping up."

"Let me guess." Connor raised a brow. "Mr. X."

"Indeed."

Connor sighed, pressing a thumb between his brows as

if to hold off a headache. "What else did you discover?"

"Mr. X has a headquarters."

"Do you know where?"

Bosko smiled grimly and turned his laptop to reveal a map. He tapped one skinny finger on the screen. "Here."

Chapter 14

I stared at the massive glass-and-steel structure. It was so modern, it seemed out of place next to the old National Museum.

"Mr. X has his headquarters in a museum?" I asked doubtfully, frowning at the monstrosity.

Connor rolled his shoulders, loosening his muscles. "If Bosko says so, then he does. He's rarely wrong."

"Seems like an odd place. People going in an out all the time. Wouldn't someone notice?"

"Look at the size of the building. There have got to be plenty of storage rooms and whatnot. Plenty of places for Mr. X to hide. It's worth a check anyway."

Tension strummed low in my belly. "Sure. You're the boss."

He grinned and pushed open the glass door. "Don't you forget it."

Inside was a large open area spread out on either side of a roped off pathway. To the left was the standard museum gift shop with posters of historic landmarks, ceramic replicas of Prague statues, and various other tchotchkes. To the right was the information desk, along with racks of maps and brochures for local attractions. The woman behind the desk spoke zero English but managed to convey that we owed some money. Three hundred koruna later, we each had tickets to the special exhibit. I was a little vague on what exhibit exactly, but she waved us away, unsmiling.

We followed the path between blue velvet ropes until it led us through an open doorway into the first room of the exhibit. It was a macabre display of various ways of executing someone, from a hanging rope to an electric chair.

"What the fuck?" I hissed.

"Interesting choice," Connor said dryly. "No wonder Mr. X likes it here."

I snorted. "Speaking of, how are we going to find Mr. X? We can't just go poking around. Security is everywhere."

Connor glanced at the old man standing next to the doorway leading to the next room of the exhibit. He wore a blue vest and name tag over his street clothes, identifying him as museum personnel. He had to be at least eighty.

"Security? You're kidding, right?"

I gave him an irritated look. "He could call the police

and then what? You can't just beat up an innocent old man."

"That's easy enough. Any time we find a door that needs investigating, one of us distracts the guard and the other has a look. Might take a while, but I bet we can inspect this whole place before dark."

"Fine." It was as good a plan as any.

It took three exhibit rooms before we found an unmarked door. Since it was partially hidden behind a display of an autopsy table covered in fake blood, I was pretty sure we weren't supposed to go rummaging around in there. The guard in that room was another ancient man in a blue vest. Connor nudged me toward him. With an eye roll, I walked up to the man and gave him my perkiest smile.

"*Ahoj,*" I said, greeting him with the only Czech word I knew. "Hello. Do you speak English?"

He did. Badly.

"What's this?" I asked, pointing to one of the pieces of the exhibit. In order to look at it, he had to turn his back on Connor and the door.

"Oh, this very interesting." The old man spent a good several minutes trying to explain to me in broken English what the thing was. I had no idea what he was trying to say, but I kept asking questions, nodding, and smiling a lot. It seemed like ages before Connor suddenly appeared beside me, and I managed to extricate myself.

"Anything?" I asked as we passed through to the next room.

"Just a storeroom. Cleaning supplies, mostly."

"Damn."

"Let's head upstairs," he suggested. "I think we'll have more luck there."

We repeated the process on the next floor with no better luck. By the time we finished the last room of the exhibit, it was dark outside.

"What now?" I asked.

Connor stopped in front of a door next to the elevator. It was marked with a fire escape sign and clearly led to a stairwell.

"Now we go to the top floor. I'm guessing that's where the offices are. Maybe we'll find someone there."

"And stick out like sore thumbs in the process. If we get caught..."

"You worry too much," he said. "If we do get caught, we play dumb tourist. No one will suspect a thing."

Sure enough, the upper floor held a warren of offices, cubicles, closets, and small storage spaces. It was all very grim and utilitarian, with bright fluorescent lights overhead and walls painted an utterly depressing grayish-white. A couple of museum posters—probably from the gift shop downstairs—hung neatly on one wall as if someone had tried to cheer up the place. It wasn't cheerful. The metallic scent of copier toner hung heavy in the air. Nearby, someone in one of the small offices was having a phone conversation that sounded intense, but it was hard to tell what with not speaking the language. A long bank of windows gave an incredible view down the hill to the old town below, the one bright spot in an otherwise oppressive place.

"This isn't it," Connor muttered. "It's too open. Exposed. No way would Mr. X set himself up here."

"Unless maybe he works here."

He slid me a look. "Possible but unlikely."

"Is there another floor?"

"No. So unless he's set up on the roof..." He trailed off as if suddenly struck by a thought.

"What?" I prodded. "What is it?"

He turned to me, eyes lit with excitement. "The basement. We haven't seen any space large enough to store the amount of display items this place must own. I'll bet you anything the museum has a basement for just that purpose. It would be a perfect place for Mr. X to set up shop undetected."

"Well, let's go." I pushed through the fire door and into the stairwell, taking the stairs as fast as I could. I could feel it. We were nearing the answer. My heart pounded with equal parts excitement and dread.

Sure enough, when we hit the ground floor landing, there was another flight of stairs leading down. Connor reached out to stop me.

"You need a weapon," he said. "You can't go in there unarmed."

We hadn't been able to take weapons through airport security, so I had no idea where he thought I'd get one. I opened my mouth to tell him so when he handed me a wicked looking dagger. The blade was black and looked incredibly sharp. I noticed he had a similar knife.

"Ceramic," he explained. "Only way to get it through security. It's far stronger than steel, sharper too, but it has a flaw. It's pretty useless against bone. The only way to end a vamp with this thing is to stab it through the heart without hitting a rib. Not so easy to do, but if you bleed it enough, you can weaken it, which makes it easier."

"You think there are vamps down there?"

"Since Mr. X is working with them, it's a distinct

possibility. Better to be safe than sorry, am I right?" He gave me a sexy, lopsided grin.

"Sure."

"Humans, on the other hand, are easy to kill. Slash to the throat or the brachial artery, and they're done."

My eyes widened. "Hunters don't kill humans. It's like the first rule or something." I hadn't even needed Kabita to tell me that, though she had. It was logical, as far as I was concerned. My job was to protect humanity, not slice and dice it.

Connor snorted. "Kabita and her rules. Listen, kid, what we're going into here is a life or death situation. Kill or be killed. If Mr. X has humans working for him, they're going to be just as deadly as any vamp and just as evil. Got it?"

I nodded, totally uncomfortable with the whole situation but not sure what else to do. In for a penny, in for a pound and all that.

He clapped me on the shoulder. "Let's go."

We took the last flight of stairs to the final landing, boots as silent as possible on the metal treads. Connor paused for a moment, as if listening, then shoved the heavy fire door. It swung open easily and quietly. Beyond was utter darkness.

Without a doubt, I knew the room was massive. It was as if my very breath echoed from distant walls. I couldn't see a damn thing, though. I wanted to flip on an overhead light, but that would have given us away.

A light stabbed through the darkness, lighting up stacks of cardboard boxes and wooden crates, spilling peanuts and bubble wrap everywhere. Connor had donned his dorky looking headlamp. I suddenly wished I had one. In the light from his gadget, I could see massive shelving units, lined with odd shapes, stretching into the distance. I'd been right. The place was enormous.

"Follow me," Connor whispered.

He paced to the right, knife at the ready as if he expected vampires to spring out of the darkness and rip out our throats. I shivered at the thought. We wended our way around stacks of boxes and other detritus. The place was surprisingly dusty, as if it was rarely used and never cleaned. When was the last time anyone had been down here? I saw no sign that anyone was making use of the place as a hideout. They'd have left tracks or something, surely. But Connor was working his way between the stacks, so I followed, unwilling to be left alone in the dark.

We moved ever deeper into the massive storage room

that was the museum basement. It seemed never-ending. Dust and the smell of musty old things tickled my nose. My hand ached from gripping the knife too tight. I was about to tell Connor this was all a waste of time when that awful gripping on the back of my skull stopped me in my tracks. I'd felt this sensation twice before. Both times...

"Vampire!" I shouted.

I was wrong. It wasn't just one vampire but half a dozen, and every one of them was headed right for me.

Shéa MacLeod

Chapter 15

The first vamp hit hard, driving me back against a stack of boxes. Sharp corners gouged my back before they toppled over with an ear shattering crash. I barely had time to regain my balance before the vamp's hands were around my throat, beady eyes staring hungrily at me in the dim light from Connor's lamp.

I stabbed wildly at the vamp while at the same time trying to pry its hands away from my throat. Finally I got the blade in good, ripping across its stomach and leaving a gaping wound. I almost gagged at the stench of old blood and bowel. It stank of dead, rotting carcass and other more awful things.

The vamp howled, thrusting me away from him and into the arms of a second vamp. The second vamp screeched with delight, clutching me to her scrawny chest. I could feel her ribs through her clothes. Her fangs dripped saliva as she tried to rip out my throat. I thrust an elbow into her gut, loosening her grip. Whirling to face her, I slashed across her neck, opening a vein with my blade. Thick, black blood oozed from the wound, and she screamed in fury but didn't let go of my arm. Sharp nails dug into my delicate skin. Another slash across her face, and she dropped me like a hot potato.

For a split second, I could breathe and then the rest of the nest was on me, fangs and claws grabbing and scraping while I slashed and hacked wildly, praying my knife wouldn't break.

"Connor!" I screamed. "Help me!" But he said nothing. Did nothing. What the hell was going on?

But I didn't have time to think. I was fighting for my life, and I was losing. Fangs sank into my calf. Hot blood slid down my leg as I screamed and kicked, dislodging the biter. Another vamp leaped right on top me, dragging me to the ground, and crushing me beneath his weight. I bucked, screaming until my throat was raw.

Suddenly the vamp lifted off me, and I could breathe again. I heard scuffling and then there was dust everywhere. I breathed a sigh of relief. Connor had finally gotten off his ass and done something. Renewed energy surged through me, and I scrambled to my feet, hacking and slashing with as much vigor as I could. One by one the vamps went up in poofs of dust until there was only one left.

I went to stab him in the heart, but Connor grabbed my arm. "Don't. We need to question him."

Only it wasn't Connor. "Inigo? What the hell are you doing here?" I gasped.

"Sit down before you fall down." I realized my arms and legs were shaking from adrenaline and overuse. I sank onto a nearby crate while Inigo held the vamp at the point of his blade.

"Who sent you?" he demanded.

The vamp smirked, fangs peeking out below his upper lip. He shook tangled dark hair out of his eyes. "Mr. X, of course. You know that."

"Don't be cheeky. Where is Mr. X?"

"I don't know. Not here, obviously." The vamp had a serious attitude problem. Did he not know Inigo had dusted his compatriots? With a little help from me, of course.

"Who is Mr. X?" Inigo demanded.

"Again, I don't know," the vamp said, shooting Inigo an angry look and me a hungry one. "We were ordered to kill the baby hunter. That's all I know."

"That's not helpful," Inigo snapped.

"I think he's telling the truth," I said.

"Unfortunately, I agree with you." Without another word he ran the blade through the vamp's heart, dusting it.

I wrapped my arms around myself, suddenly cold. "How did you find me?"

"I've been following you since you left London."

"Let me guess. Kabita sent you."

He smiled a little. "Good guess. She was convinced you weren't ready for the kind of fight Connor was bound to get you into."

I sighed and pinched the bridge of my nose. There was a headache lurking behind my eyes. "She was right."

"I'm surprised you can admit that."

"Hey. I'm not an idiot. I know when I'm beat. When we get back to London, I'll put everything I have into training, even if it means punching the daylights out of a bunch of stupid sandbags from now until kingdom come."

Inigo chuckled. "I think I can convince her you're beyond that."

"I'd appreciate it. Those sandbags are getting boring." I glanced around. "Where'd that asshole, Connor, go?"

Inigo shook his head, his face a mask of anger. "I saw him slip out during the fight. I'd have gone after him but helping you seemed more important at the time. What the hell is going on?"

"That's what I want to know. This is the second time

he's left me alone in a fight. Well, third, if you count Craggy Face."

"Craggy Face?"

I told him about the so-called beggar and the resulting near-mugging. "Maybe I'm wrong, but there was something really odd about the whole thing. The fact that Connor just disappeared like that. And they were talking way too long for it just to be some beggar."

"I think you're right. And I think it's time Connor MacRae answers some very serious questions."

"He's probably back at the hotel by now with some excuse about how this was a training exercise to make me a better hunter."

Inigo scowled, his blue eyes turning stormy behind his glasses. "That man is a liar."

"I'm starting to agree with you." I clambered off the crate and started for the exit. "And I'm going to find out why if I have to beat it out of him."

Inigo snorted.

"Fine. If *you* have to beat it out of him."

# # #

By the time we reached the hotel, Connor was long

gone. His room was empty, and the concierge gave me an apologetic look and a shrug, and said Mr. MacRae had checked out half an hour earlier. "You just missed him. I am so sorry." He probably thought it was a lover's breakup. He had no idea.

I turned to Inigo. "Do you suppose Connor is somehow connected to this Mr. X? That he planned for me to die?"

"It's looking like it." Inigo's expression was grim.

"But why would he do that? He's a hunter. Why would he be involved in killing other hunters?"

"Money. Power. All sorts of reasons. I say we find him and ask him."

"But how?" I wailed in frustration. "He's long gone by now."

Inigo's grin was evil. "I have my ways. Come."

He strode from the hotel, down the worn stone steps to the street. He paused a moment, as if listening for something. It was odd, but then he was Kabita's cousin. He had claimed he wasn't a hunter, but maybe he had some of her abilities. He certainly had training.

"This way." He started down the hill toward the St. Charles Bridge, with me following. Instead of turning right toward the bridge, he turned left toward the train station.

"Let me guess," I said dryly. "He's trying to get out of town. Why doesn't he just get a damn taxi to the airport?"

"Trains are easier. No real security. No sitting around waiting for a flight. Pay cash for a ticket, jump on the next train, and disappear into Eastern Europe. We'd never track him."

"Damn," I bit out.

"Exactly."

We followed whatever mysterious trail Inigo was picking up, only instead of leading into the train station, it veered off around it. Inigo stopped in front of an alley. It didn't look promising.

"Trail leads in there," he said. "We need to be on guard. More than likely, it's a trap. You should stay here."

"The hell I will. I'm the hunter here. I'm going in with you."

He sighed. "Fine. But stay close."

I nodded, and we approached the alley cautiously. I wanted to rush in, punch Connor in the face, but I got that we needed to be cautious. It was night. Who knew what sorts of creatures Connor was using. I didn't feel that gripping on the back of my head, which was a relief. No vampires, or they weren't close enough to sense. I still wasn't sure what my little early warning system was all about, but I was starting to think it was useful.

"Can you see anything?" I asked as Inigo peered around the corner of the building and into the alley, using the brick wall to protect himself.

"Nope. Just a dark alley, but I'm certain he's down there. Stay behind me." He entered the alley, sticking close to the wall, making himself as small a target as possible. I followed his lead, crouching low. It was actually harder than it seemed.

The only light was from the streetlamp behind me and the nearly full moon above. At least it had stopped raining. The huddled shapes of garbage bins lined the wall. The end was a wrought iron fence with tall spikes on top and a narrow gate in the middle, leading to the street beyond. I couldn't tell if it was locked or not or why there'd be a gate at one end and not the other. Inigo was right. This had to be a trap. I opened my mouth to say something when a figure stepped out from behind one of the bins.

"Well, well, well. If it isn't the baby hunter. Let me guess. Mr. Jones saved you from the big bad vampires."

"Connor, you son of a bitch. I'm going to kick your ass," I snarled, starting forward, but Inigo yanked me back. Naturally that made me angrier, but I managed not to punch him. He was on my side, after all.

Connor let out what could only be described as a mocking laugh. "God, you are so predictable. No wonder the vamps had no trouble taking you all out."

"Hunters, you mean."

I couldn't see his face, but I could hear the snarl in his voice. "You aren't hunters. None of you. Pathetic wastes are what you are. *I'm* a hunter, trained from birth."

"So you're killing hunters because you're *jealous?*" Was he really that insane?

"I don't think that's the reason," Inigo said calmly. He was still blocking me from anything Connor might pull. I wasn't sure whether to be grateful for his protection or irritated because he thought I couldn't protect myself. Unfortunately, he was probably right, if my previous run-ins with vamps were anything to go by. One of these days, though, I was going to be so badass, I would be the one protecting him.

"At least you've got a few brain cells to rub together, Jones." Connor seemed relaxed. Clearly he wasn't in a hurry. "More than I can say for most."

"Then why are you doing it?" I asked.

"You really can't figure it out?" he taunted.

I mulled over what little I knew about hunters. Kabita had said the murdered people were *potential* hunters. "You don't want the hunters to come into their power," I guessed, "but I don't understand why. You're a hunter. We're all on the same side. This can't be about you feeling threatened. That's just... stupid."

Connor snorted. "Well, at least you got that last part right. No, this isn't about me feeling threatened. This is about me being tired of the hunter game. I want more for myself than an endless life hunting vamps and demons." There was something in his tone that gave me the shivers.

"How is killing potential hunters going to accomplish that?" Inigo asked.

Connor moved slightly, and the moonlight revealed the wicked cast to his features. Suddenly he didn't look handsome. He looked almost ugly. How had I never noticed before?

"There are certain powerful people in this world that would prefer hunters cease to exist. Particularly"—he paused, eyeing me—"those they can't control."

"So, what?" I asked. "You're trying to prove yourself to them by getting your vamp lapdogs to take out hunters? How could you turn on your own kind like that?"

"Easy. They offered me a lot of money." His lips twisted into a sardonic smile.

"That's evil," I sputtered.

He threw back his head and laughed. "You think I'm the only one who wants to stop the hunters? I'm not. There are plenty out there who want to end hunter existence."

That thought chilled me to the bone. "Why did I survive?" I had to know.

He shrugged, seemingly unconcerned. "I don't know. You weren't supposed to, but you're different somehow. Which is why killing you is going to be so much fun."

Shéa MacLeod

Chapter 16

Connor moved in a blur, sending Inigo flying into a dumpster with a sickening crash. Then he turned on me, eyes black in the moonlight. "Sorry, kid, but I can't let you live. I've got too much riding on this." He didn't sound sorry.

I slid the ceramic blade he'd given me from my back pocket. "Stop calling me kid." I lashed out with the knife, slashing him deep across the upper arm.

He jerked back and stared at me in surprise. Then he smirked. "Bravo. Lucky shot."

"If that's what you think, you're an idiot." I was not an expert, but Kabita had been training me. I knew a thing or two.

He snorted. "After how many times I've had to save your ass? I doubt that."

I dodged in time to avoid his boot to my knee. Using my momentum, I darted around him and sliced along his ribs, making sure not to cut so deep I hit bone. I saw the darker stain of blood spread against his lighter colored jacket. He snarled and struck out, catching my wrist. My knife flew out of nerveless fingers and skittered over the cobblestones. I glanced to Inigo for help, but he was crumpled on the ground, unmoving. *Shit.* I was on my own.

A knife flashed in Connor's hand. It was a lot bigger than mine. More like a bowie knife. He advanced on me, slashing and hacking, barely missing with each swipe. Sweat beaded my forehead and upper lip, and slid down my spine. I was growing tired, but all I could do was keep dancing out of the way. And then my back hit the iron bars of the gate at the end of the alley hard enough to rattle teeth. I had nowhere else to go.

His grin was evil. "Any last words?"

"Sure." I tilted my chin up, daring him. "Bite me."

And I did what any woman in my situation would do. I kicked him in the balls. Hard.

Connor hit the ground with a high pitched scream. I didn't wait. I kicked again, this time in the face. I heard the satisfying, albeit sickening, crunch of cartilage as his nose broke. His scream this time was gurgled as blood flowed down his face. I knew my strength was in my legs, so I kept kicking, hitting ribs, arms, and I don't know what else. I kept it up until Connor lay on the cobblestones, bleeding and mewling. He was pathetic. I lifted my boot to strike again, still beyond furious.

"Stop."

I glanced up. Inigo stood on the other side of Connor's inert body. "You've done enough. He's down."

"The bastard killed a whole bunch of hunters," I snapped.

"And he'll pay for it, believe me. But not at your hand. That's not your job."

I screamed in frustration. "My job sucks."

He laughed softly. "Yeah. Sometimes it does."

"Who's going to make him pay? The cops?"

He shook his head. "Not the locals, no. A very special kind of cop. Go wait for me on the street, okay?"

I glared down at Connor. "But—"

"Go." There was a command in his voice that stiffened my spine and compelled me to obey.

I stomped to the entrance of the alley but refused to go one step farther. I heard Inigo on the phone, talking low. I couldn't make out the words. I wasn't even sure he was speaking English.

Finally there was an odd flash of light and then Inigo appeared at the entrance of the alley. "Let's go."

"But Connor—"

"It's taken care of." His tone was far grimmer than I'd ever heard.

I opened my mouth to question him, but the look on his face stopped me. Instead I asked, "What about you? Are you all right? You hit that dumpster pretty hard."

"I'm tougher than I look," he assured me. "You did well tonight," he said, taking my arm and steering me away from the alley. "I'm proud of you. Kabita will be too when she hears you took down a corrupt hunter."

I was proud of me, too. For the first time, I'd gone head-to-head with someone better trained and more powerful, and I'd come out on top. "Somehow I don't think Kabita will be surprised Connor turned out evil."

"She never did like that guy."

# # #

"I never did like that guy." Kabita paced back and forth in front of the training ring.

"Yeah, that's what Inigo said." I grinned as I slammed one fist into a sandbag. The thing flew through the air until the chain snapped, and it smacked against the far wall before slumping to the floor in a pathetic heap.

"Always full of himself. Always willing to cross the line when it suited him." She shook her head. "Rat bastard."

She was definitely pissed if she was using language that

blue. "What will happen to him?"

She looked surprised that I asked. "You didn't see? Inigo didn't tell you?"

"See what? Inigo said he was going to get some special kind of police to deal with Connor and sent me out of the alley. He was on the phone, then there was a flash of light. He said it was taken care of. That was all. I'd like to know his punishment. I think I deserve that."

Kabita's expression was grim. "There is only one punishment for a hunter who murders other hunters like MacRae did."

I suddenly felt queasy. "I'm guessing it's not one you come back from."

"No." There was a finality in her tone that told me Connor was dead. I had a feeling Inigo had had something to do with it, but I wasn't sure what or how, and it was clear Kabita wouldn't be answering that question. I wasn't even sure I wanted to know.

I cleared my throat. "Connor said there were others out there. Other people who wanted hunters dead."

She nodded. "There always are. People seeking power or fame or whatever stupid damn thing. Don't worry. We've got people on it."

"We?"

She raised one black eyebrow. "You ask a lot of questions."

"There's a lot I don't know, and if I'm going to survive, I think it's important to learn about this stuff. Don't you?"

She mulled it over. "Yes. Eventually. But right now what's important is learning to protect yourself. Learning to hunt and kill the vamps so when the time comes, you'll be ready."

For now, I'd let it go. But one day, she was going to tell me. I grinned. "Well, then, let's get to it, shall we?"

Chapter 17

"Inigo called." Kabita set a plate of eggs and ham in front of me.

I needed a lot of protein these days. Training had been going well, and I was starting to see a lot of muscle definition beneath the fluff. I felt stronger than I ever had. More confident. I liked it.

"Really? How's he doing?" It had been two months since Inigo had returned to the US, and I had resumed training with Kabita. I wasn't always thrilled with it, but I knew it was important. We'd even done a couple of real hunts together, and I'd dusted three vamps all on my own. Kabita hadn't had to save me even once.

She filled her plate before sitting across from me. "I know you love it here in London, but how do you feel about your hometown?"

I frowned. "Portland? It's a fantastic place, of course, but I live here now. Why?"

"We've had a job offer."

I blinked. "We?"

She nodded. "You. Me. Inigo."

"What kind of job offer?"

"The American government has a clandestine division called the SRA, the Supernatural Regulatory Agency. Sort of like the FBI or the CIA, but for supernatural stuff. They're a small agency with a limited number of agents, so they hire freelancers, hunters like us to set up shop in certain areas around the country to monitor supernatural activity and protect the local populace from vampires and such."

"And they want us to take over the Portland area?"

She nodded. "They just had a spot open up. There's a cover already in place. We just move in and do our thing."

"What happened to the last hunter?" I asked, though I was pretty sure I already knew.

"What usually happens to hunters? He was killed in the line of duty."

I grimaced. "And we're going to take over. Fun."

"It's what we do," she said calmly. "It's going to be rough, especially at first, but it should be interesting. You in?"

Hunt vamps on my home turf? Kick vamp ass on a daily basis? "Hell, yeah. I'm in." I held up my coffee cup. "To Portland."

Kabita rolled her eyes but joined me. "To Portland."

The End

Want to read more about Morgan's adventures as a vampire hunter? Check out the international bestselling book that started it all: *Kissed by Darkness (Sunwalker Saga – Book 1).*

Keep reading for the Bonus Short Story
Irish Kiss

Irish Kiss

"You can't be serious." I gave Kabita a death glare across her desk before returning my attention to our prospective client, who was lounging in the chair next to me.

In the months since we'd moved from London to Portland, Oregon, many strange people had walked through the doors of Kabita Jones's private investigation firm, where I worked as a vampire hunter, demon spawn slayer, and general bad-guy ass-kicker. But this guy pretty much took the cake for weirdness.

"Oh, I am quite serious, I assure you." He folded his hands calmly over his slightly rounded stomach and returned my glare measure-for-measure from under his bushy red eyebrows.

"You want us to find your…" I couldn't say it. I really couldn't say it. "Pot of gold," I finally choked out. It was all I could do not to bust a gut laughing. I'd finally heard it all. Next he'd want me to follow a damned rainbow or something.

"Yes. I want you to find my pot of gold."

"Mr. O'Leery is one of the Leprechauns, Morgan,"

Kabita interrupted. Her voice was calm and even, but her eyes promised murder and mayhem if I didn't behave. She was probably afraid I'd open my big mouth and say something stupid. She was right to be worried.

I eyeballed him. "You don't look like a leprechaun." Actually, he looked pretty much exactly like a leprechaun, except that he was nearly six feet tall, and wearing jeans and a gray cable-knit sweater. I was just trying to be nice.

He heaved a sigh that spoke of long-suffering. "What do you expect a Leprechaun to look like? Short, red beard, green suit, holding a shoe?"

He'd pretty much nailed it. I mean, come on, we've all seen the Lucky Charms guy, right? Okay, Lucky didn't have a beard, but still.

Our new client looked nothing like the Lucky Charms guy. Not only was Mr. O'Leery too tall, there wasn't a speck of green in sight. No beard, either. Heck, he didn't even sound Irish.

"Okay, fine, so you're a leprechaun…"

"Leprechaun," he corrected.

"What?"

"Capital 'L'. Like American."

I blinked. "Excuse me?" How the hell could he hear whether I capitalized a word or not?

He heaved another long-suffering sigh. "I'm not one of those moronic fairytale people you humans like to make fun of. I am Leprechaun, and I've come to you because I need your help. Now are you going to help me or not?"

Render me speechless. I glanced at Kabita, who gave me a slight nod. "Of course," I gave him my best professional smile. "That's what we do."

"Good," he said with a slight nod.

"Right." I settled back in my seat. "When was the last time you saw your, um, property?" I couldn't say pot of gold. I just couldn't.

"Last Tuesday."

I blinked. "You waited a week to come see us?" If I'd lost a pot of gold, I certainly wouldn't be dilly-dallying around. I'd have called the cops. Scratch that—I'd have called my friends and fellow crime solvers, Kabita and Inigo. I'd have had the whole gang on the case within minutes.

"Well, I know who has it," O'Leery admitted.

Kabita and I exchanged looks.

"You do?" Her voice was just this side of testy. Kabita did not like when clients withheld important details.

"Oh, yes. I thought I would try to recover it myself.

Unfortunately, I didn't have any luck."

I really, honestly tried to keep a straight face. I swear I did, but I couldn't help the smile that spread across my face. "Right, you lost your luck."

His eyes narrowed. "Don't be ridiculous. The pot of gold has nothing to do with luck. I'm not talking about some ridiculous children's story."

This from a leprechaun. Excuse me. That would be "Leprechaun."

"Fine, so who has your gold? And if you know who took it, why didn't you have any luck getting it back from him? Or her." If he beat around the bush anymore, I swore I'd grab the stapler off Kabita's desk and bash him over the head with it. Why clients always insisted on being clever and mysterious was beyond me. If you want a crime solved, being clever and mysterious is not the way to get it done.

O'Leery leaned forward in his chair and glanced around the office like he thought men in black might come popping out of the walls or something. "I'm pretty sure it was the mermaid."

"Excuse me?"

"She's had it in for me for ages," he said, as if that explained everything.

Seriously? I needed a drink. A really big drink. Or maybe I needed to go back to bed and pretend this day had never happened.

"What mermaid and why does she have it in for you?"

O'Leery gave me a glare that clearly said he thought I was thick in the head. "The one down at Fringe." He named the local club frequented by members of the supernatural set. "We used to date, you know."

Now I could say see why a woman who used to date O'Leery might want to key his car or TP his house or set his garden gnomes on fire, but steal his pot of gold? He must have done something really bad.

"You tried to get it back from her, and she wouldn't give it to you," I said.

"She claimed she didn't have it. Obviously she's lying." His voice dripped with disdain.

Kabita and I exchanged another look.

"Exactly how did she steal the gold, Mr. O'Leery?" Kabita finally asked the burning question.

How on earth would a mermaid get out of a fish tank and steal a pot of gold presumably stored on land? For that matter, how could the two of them... ew, never mind. The thought made my stomach turn.

"Well, obviously she grew legs," he said as if such a

thing happened every day.

"Mr. O'Leery," Kabita's voice took on an edge I was familiar with. She was at the end of her patience. "Mermaids cannot grow legs."

Kabita was right. The whole mermaids-growing-legs thing? Total myth. They couldn't breathe on land either. Like fish, they could only breathe underwater.

"No doubt she had help," O'Leery said obstinately.

"So you have no actual proof your ex-girlfriend stole your gold?" I asked, already knowing the answer.

"She must have done it."

Damn, he was stubborn. "Okay, fine. You're probably right. She probably did it." I decided to humor him. "But let's just suppose for a minute somebody else might have had something to do with it. Helped her, maybe. Who else might have done it?"

He tugged at his lower lip, a frown creasing his forehead. "Well, there's that sorcerer."

Kabita flipped open her laptop and started tapping at the keys. "Which sorcerer, Mr. O'Leery?" She had a database of witches, sorcerers, and magic practitioners in the area, which wasn't entirely surprising, seeing as how Kabita was a natural born witch. Something I'd only recently learned.

"What's his name…Megatron."

We both stared at O'Leery, our mouths hanging half-open. I was pretty certain there weren't any sorcerers anywhere in the world named Megatron. If there was, the guy needed to rethink his moniker.

Kabita peered at her screen and tapped a few more keys. "Do you mean Margeon?"

"Ah, yes." O'Leery nodded. "That's the one."

What the hell kind of name was Margeon? "Um, why would this Margeon guy steal your gold?"

"He's my neighbor."

"And?"

"And I might have accidentally killed some of his roses."

I rolled my eyes. Great. A pissing match between a leprechaun—excuse me, Leprechaun—and a sorcerer over gardening. That was all I needed.

"Anyone else?" I was half afraid to ask.

"Well…" He hesitated.

"Spill it, O'Leery."

"There's this vampire, you see." He shifted in his seat nervously. "He might have a slight grudge against me."

I narrowed my eyes. "Why?"

"I might have sort of cheated him at cards."

That was a new one. "Vampires don't play cards." They cared about one thing: drinking human blood. Playing cards wasn't in the cards, so to speak.

"This was while he was still alive."

Oh, hell. It wasn't just any grudge, then. Not if the vamp had carried it over into undeath. Shit. I did not like this case, not one little bit. "You got the vamp's address?"

O'Leery gave it to me. "You'll help me then? You'll find my pot of gold?"

I glanced over at Kabita, shrugged, then turned back to our new client. "Yeah, we'll help you."

"Excellent. You'd best get to work then. Time's wasting." And with that he was out the door before I could catch my breath.

A Leprechaun. Fabulous. Must be my lucky day.

* * *

I decided to hit Fringe first. It was midafternoon, which meant the club would still be closed. Fortunately, one of the bartenders lived above the club. He knew me. Sort of.

I stopped in front of a blue door sandwiched between the club's entrance and the travel agent next door. The button for the doorbell was half hidden behind some planter thing filled with what looked like dead geraniums. I pressed it. One quick ring, nice and polite.

I waited. Nothing. So I gave it another quick ring, just in case. Still nothing. I leaned on the bell.

From somewhere inside, I heard a thump, followed by a crash, followed by a few more thumps and a whole lot of cussing. Finally the door swung open, and I was greeted with a snarled, "What?"

"Hey, Nate. How's it going?"

He glared at me, squinting in the afternoon sun. "Was going fine until you showed up."

Nate wasn't a large man. He was wiry and quick, with a ridiculously sharp memory recall, which made him an excellent bartender. He was an average-looking guy with dark hair cropped short and intelligent brown eyes. He hadn't bothered taking off last night's eyeliner; it was smudged around his eyes, making him look like a raccoon.

"What do you want?"

"Come on, Nate, is that any way to treat a friend?"

"It's way too early in the fu—"

"I just need to talk to the mermaid," I said, interrupting him.

He squinted at me as though I'd lost my mind. "Morgan, mermaids don't talk."

"Yeah, I know, but you have to communicate with her somehow, right?"

He frowned. "Not really. The Boss sort of takes care of all that. The rest of the time, she just swims around in that damn tank."

"I'll figure it out, but I need to talk to her. Please?"

I wasn't going to get into an argument with Nate over the morality of keeping a living, intelligent being locked up in what amounted to a giant fish tank. I'd seen her before on my visits to Fringe, and nobody, least of all the mermaid, had ever seemed bothered about it. I'd have to ask Kabita. Maybe she knew something about the situation.

I finally managed to convince Nate to let me into the club for a few minutes. He didn't know the mermaid's name or anything about her, and he claimed he'd never seen O'Leery before. I had no idea how O'Leery had managed a relationship with the mermaid if she never left the club, and he'd never been there. Guess I'd have to ask her. If I could figure out how to communicate with a being who couldn't talk.

Nate flipped on a few low lights and left me to do my

thing while he messed around behind the bar. I slowly approached the giant tank, which took up most of one wall of the club. Inside, I could just make out the curled form of the mermaid. She was still, as though sleeping, her arms wrapped around her chest, her long hair waving gently in the water.

I pressed my face close to the glass like a little kid. I'd never gotten a really good look at her before. The club had always been too crowded.

She basically looked like you'd expect a mermaid to look. Girl on the top half, fish on the bottom. Her long tail was covered in scales that shimmered ever so slightly in the dim light of the club. I knew from before that her scales were purple and blue with hints of green, just like her hair. Her skin was milky white. I could even see the blue veins just under the pale flesh.

Suddenly her eyes flew open, and I found myself staring into a pair of golden orbs. I'm talking true gold. Like the metal. The eyes were flat, expressionless, and very not human. Frankly, they freaked me out.

"Um, hello," I kept my face close to the glass and my voice low. I knew fish were sensitive to sound, and that sound carried underwater. I had no idea if mermaids were as sensitive as fish.

She opened her mouth, peeled back her lips, and hissed at me like a freaking cat. Her mouth was full of razor-sharp teeth, like the kind found in predators. So mermaids weren't the pretty fairy princesses of the underwater kingdom, after all. I'd hate to think what her idea of a good meal was.

"Sorry to wake you," I tried again, "but my name is Morgan Bailey, and I'm a private investigator. I need to ask you a few questions."

She hissed again and made a run—er, swim—for the glass. My instinct was to pull back, but I held my ground. I knew I was safe on my side of the glass. With a sneer, she whipped away, deeper into the tank. I stared after her, wondering what to do next.

"She doesn't understand you, you know."

The voice that interrupted my thoughts was light, feminine, but not necessarily female. Definitely not Nate. I turned around, but the speaker was well hidden in the shadows.

"Sorry, who are you?" I asked.

I made out the vague wave of a hand and still wasn't sure if it was a woman's or a man's. "This is my place."

"You're the Boss." The one Nate and the other bouncers always talked about but no one had ever seen.

"Yes. The Boss. I like that."

I could almost hear the smile in their voice. "I'm sorry for intruding, but I'm…"

"Morgan Bailey, private investigator. Vampire hunter."

I frowned. "Yeah. That's right. How did you…?"

"How did I know? I know a great many things. I also know you don't speak Merr, so you will never be able to communicate with our little friend there."

"But you can," I said.

"Of course."

"And if I tell you what I need to know, can you ask her for me?"

There was a pause. "Perhaps. It depends on the questions."

"I have a client named O'Leery. He claims he's—" I paused. The whole thing was so ridiculous. "He claims the mermaid is his ex, and she stole something from him."

There was a light chuckle from deep within the shadows. "Oh, yes. Mr. O'Leery. He claims, I believe, that our little friend stole his pot of gold."

"That's right. Frankly I don't understand how a mermaid and a Leprechaun can possibly have a relationship to begin with, let alone enough of one that she'd steal from him." I shrugged. "Still, I have to ask."

"Of course."

There was a moment of silence, followed by a strange humming sound which made the hairs on the back of my neck stand up and goosebumps break out all over my arms. Freaky, that's what it was. Spooky.

The humming stopped and the Boss spoke again. "It is true Mr. O'Leery and she were once a couple, but that has been over for many years. She has not left this tank. She has not touched Mr. O'Leery's gold, and she does not know who has or where it is now."

"She didn't maybe hire someone or, uh, something?"

Another chuckle. "No."

I didn't know if I could trust the Boss or not, but frankly, I didn't have much of a choice. It was obvious the mermaid wasn't going to speak to me, even if I had been able to speak Merr. "Okay. Thanks for your time. I very much appreciate it."

"Not a problem," said the Boss. "Anytime. Anytime at all, Morgan Bailey."

I left the club as quickly as possible, without making it obvious, and took a deep breath of fresh air the minute I was outside. The Boss had totally freaked me out. I'd be quite happy if I never saw him, or her, or it, again.

* * *

Since it was still light out, I decided to visit the sorcerer first before heading to the vampire's nest. Last thing I needed was for my person of interest to go up in flames before I had a chance to question him.

As I got into my car, my phone rang. It was Inigo, the third member of our investigation team and Kabita's cousin.

"Kabita tells me you have a new client. You going to ask for your three wishes when you find his pot of gold?" He was all but laughing out loud.

"Very funny."

"Seriously, is there anything I can do to help?"

I almost said no but figured I might as well put him to good use. "Yeah. Can you check with local pawn shops, see if anyone has brought in a large amount of gold recently?"

"Like a big pot of it?" He went off into gales of laughter.

I rolled my eyes. He could be so juvenile. "Oh, you are very funny. Can you do it?"

"Sure thing. Let you know what I find out." He was

still laughing when we hung up.

I gave Kabita a quick call. "It's a no-go on the mermaid angle. Have you found out anything about this Margeon character?"

"Not a lot," Kabita admitted. "His real name is Melvin Smith, and he's from Omaha. He works for the Walmart out in Troutdale."

"No wonder he changed his name to Margeon. Does he have any real abilities?"

"Hard to say." I could hear her tapping on her keyboard as she spoke. "He's pretty new to the area, and he keeps to himself, mostly. He's a low-level member of the local sorcerer's guild, but that could just be because he's new. So be cautious."

"Roger that."

* * *

Melvin Smith—er, Margeon—lived in outer Southeast Portland. It had once been a nice, lower-middle-class neighborhood of small but cozy houses with large yards and friendly neighbors. In recent years the gangs and drug dealers had moved in. Now the small houses were more run-down than cozy, and the large yards grown out of control. Don't even get me started on the neighbors.

Margeon's house was just off the main street on a quiet side road. It was a typical neighborhood for the area, with the usual '60s-style ranch houses. Paint peeled almost completely off the walls, cracks laced the windows, and a couple had doors with gaping holes in the paneling. I wondered if they'd been kicked in by the police or the criminals. If I hadn't been a hunter, I think I'd have been a little nervous visiting Margeon's street.

The sorcerer from Nebraska's house stood out with its neatly trimmed lawn and fresh coat of paint. It was sandwiched between two of the worst looking houses on the block. I wondered which one was the Leprechaun's until I saw the dead rosebushes along the East side of the property. Bingo.

I parked my car in the drive and strolled nice and slow to the front door. A couple of less-than-savory types eyeballed the Mustang from across the street so I did the one thing guaranteed to make them think I was a crazy person.

I walked back to the car and popped the trunk. Inside was my hunting gear: UV guns, knives, swords, machetes. You know, the fun stuff.

In plain view of the two men, I started pulling out and

inspecting my little arsenal. Only the blades were deadly to humans, but they didn't know that. Out of the corner of my eye, I could see they were getting more and more interested. I pulled my *dao* out of its sheath and held it up to the light, giving the sword few flicks and slashes. Then I turned and caught the men's gaze.

I smiled and let the hunter inside me creep into my eyes. The cold look that spoke of killing and death.

That did it. The two couldn't get out of there fast enough. With a laugh I carefully placed the blade back in the trunk and slammed the lid shut.

I can't explain my hunter side. It just is. Some kind of weird superpower which made me stronger and faster than a normal than other humans. Kabita claimed it was a genetic anomaly. Why I lucked out is anyone's guess, but it was who I was. I'd learned to embrace it. More or less.

I rapped on Margeon's door. I heard some shuffling inside before the door cracked open. A pale hazel eye in a pasty-white face appeared in the crack just above the safety chain. "What do you want?" They should have been forceful words, but coming from Margeon, they were anything but.

I decided address him as Melvin probably wouldn't get me far. "Margeon?"

The eye widened. "Who are you? How do you know my name?" The eye narrowed. "If you've come here to put a hex on me, it will fail!" His voice wobbled a little on the last.

"Uh, I'm not a witch, so no hexes, I promise."

He seemed to think about that. "All right. What do you want?"

"May I come in?"

"No way!" he gasped. "You might steal a lock of my hair or my toothbrush or something."

I stared at him, baffled. "Why would I do that?"

"To give to a witch so she can put a hex on me."

Riiiight. "My name is Morgan Bailey, and I'm a private detective. I just need to ask you a couple questions."

"Private detective? What do you want with me?"

"It's about your neighbor, Mr. O'Leery."

Margeon's eyes widened even further, if that was possible. "That son of a newt? Do you know what he did? He killed my Andenken an Alma de lAigle."

"I'm sorry. Your what?"

"My rosebushes." The fury in his voice was obvious. And loud.

Hoo-boy, loony on the loose. "Yeah, he told me you think that. So I was wondering, did you decide to take revenge on Mr. O'Leery for the death of your rosebushes?"

"Of course I did. What kind of a sorcerer would I be if I didn't take revenge?" There was an almost maniacal gleam in the one eye I could see. The rest of him was still firmly ensconced behind the door.

"What form did your revenge take?"

"I cursed him, of course."

I almost choked. "Really? What kind of curse?"

He grinned. "I cursed his hair so it would all fall out."

"Oh, excellent curse. Excellent." It obviously hadn't worked. Last time I'd seen O'Leery, he'd had a very full and luxurious head of hair. "You didn't happen to take your revenge in any other way, did you?"

He frowned. "Like what?"

"Like steal something of his maybe?"

He drew himself up to his full height, which was a good three inches shorter than my five-foot–five, and bellowed indignantly, "I did no such thing! Sorcerers do not steal. Rule Number 96."

I'd never heard of any such sorcerer rules. In fact, the few sorcerers I'd run into hadn't exactly been full of scruples. Still, Margeon seemed very convinced of said rule, so who was I to crush him? "Okay, thanks, Mr.

Sm...uh, Margeon." I turned to go.

"Do you work for O'Leery?" he called after me.

Shit. I turned around. "Yes, Mr. O'Leery did hire me."

There was a shriek of outrage, and the door slammed shut. I stood there for a moment, blinking in shock before the door was ripped open again, revealing Melvin Smith in all his Margeon the Sorcerer glory.

I wanted to laugh, I really did. The guy was wearing a burgundy velvet bathrobe to which someone had sewn (rather badly) some sort of fake fur trim. On his feet were a pair of blue-and-gold satin slippers, the kind that curl up at the toes like something out of Arabian Nights. But the crowning glory was on his head: a tinfoil "wizard's hat" with stickers of suns and moons and stars.

He stormed out onto the front porch and waved around what looked like a stick from a drum set. I could only assume it was supposed to be his wand. Then Margeon screamed at the top of his lungs. I had no idea what he was saying, but it didn't sound good.

I'm only mildly ashamed to admit I turned tail and ran for my car. Once I had driven far enough away from crazy Melvin Smith, I pulled out my cell and rang Kabita.

"I think that Melvin/Margeon guy just put a curse on me."

Kabita snorted. "Doubtful."

"Yeah?"

"Yeah. I had a word with the guild. Apparently good old Margeon is a bit of a wing-nut. He has zero powers, but he's absolutely convinced he's the next Merlin."

"You've got to be kidding me." I started laughing. "Why on earth did they let him in, then?"

"They were afraid he'd start blabbing if they didn't," she said. "The last thing they need is that kind of notoriety. When he showed up, claiming to be descended from a long line of powerful sorcerers, they brought him in and made him swear an oath of silence. They've been keeping him busy writing a *Sorcerer's Code of Ethics* or some such thing."

That explained Rule Number 96. I was relieved I didn't have to worry about my hair falling out.

"Any luck with O'Leery's gold?" Kabita asked.

"Not yet," I admitted. "But I've still got one more suspect to interview."

"Let me guess. The vampire."

I sighed. "Naturally." I was used to killing vamps, not questioning them.

"Maybe you should take Inigo with you."

I frowned. "Why? You think I can't handle a vampire

178

on my own?"

"Sure you can. But you don't want to kill him before you have a chance to question him. Inigo can hold him down while you beat him up." I could hear her laughter on the other end. "Besides, where you're going, you could use some backup."

She was being a dope, but she had a point. I could take a vamp, no problem. But that was if I wanted him dead. If I wanted him alive, well, that was a different ballgame. It would be easier if I had some help. "Okay, I'll call Inigo," I finally said with some reluctance.

"No need. I'll have him meet you there."

"Fabulous."

* * *

Inigo was waiting for me when I arrived at the home of the last person of interest. I use the term "home" loosely, since it was actually an abandoned auto body shop in one of the rougher areas of town. And by "rougher," I mean it made Melvin's neighborhood look downright Mayberry.

I hated that my heart skipped a tiny beat when I saw Inigo leaning up against his car. All lean and broad shouldered and shaggy haired with those brilliant blue eyes shining behind the lenses of his nerd glasses. He was the stuff dreams were made of, but he was off limits. Big time. Not only was he Kabita's cousin, but he was far too young for me.

"Hey, Morgan." His voice it was smooth as velvet with the faintest hint of a British accent. I refused to melt like butter. I needed to stay focused, not swoon all over the unattainable.

"Inigo." I gave him a brief nod. "Kabita told you the plan?"

He smirked like he was having a little too much fun. "Go in, hold him down while you beat the truth out of him, then dust his ass."

"Yeah, pretty much." It was a simple plan, as plans went, but one of the first things you learned as a hunter is that things didn't always go according to plan. "I take it there's a back door."

He nodded. "Side door, actually. Looks like that's what he's been using. The garage door is still padlocked, and the one in front looks like it hasn't been opened in years."

Normally I wouldn't worry about leaving one door unguarded, but it was quickly approaching twilight. I wouldn't put it past the vamp to make a run for it. "Do you think you can open it?" I nodded at the front door. Inigo was right. There was plant life growing up through the cracks in the pavement in front of it, and the doorknob looked rusted through.

He shot me a look, one I could only interpret as "duh."

"Fine. Wait for thirty, then go in. I'll hit the side door." I didn't wait for his reply. I knew he'd be ready when I was. Inigo had saved my life once before in Prague. I knew I could trust him to have my back.

The side door definitely showed signs of regular use. This was it. The little gripping sensation at the back of my skull confirmed it, my hunter senses letting me know a vampire was near.

I took a deep breath, counted to three, then shoved open the door. The inside of the old auto body shop was nearly pitch black. I couldn't see or hear anything, but my "other" senses were definitely screaming at me, so I knew the vamp was inside somewhere, waiting.

I heard the front door screech open on rusty hinges, and light from the streetlamps spilled across the dusty floor. The light was blocked momentarily as Inigo moved through the doorway into the room.

I edged across the floor cautiously, straining to catch

the slightest sound. There was nothing. Silent as the tomb. I stepped a little farther into the room. Inigo mirrored me, his body a dark shape against the outside light.

A big, black something dropped from the ceiling right on top of Inigo. The thing was man-shaped, and I watched in horror as a pair of fangs flashed before sinking into the side of Inigo's neck.

Inigo let out a roar and tried to shake the thing off, but the vamp clung like superglue. Inigo might be wily and strong, but when something is on your back, wily and strong goes right out the window.

I darted across the floor, but before I could get to them, Inigo had rammed himself into a wall. I heard a couple of the vamp's vertebrae make sickening pops, but that didn't seem to faze the thing. It still had its fangs buried in Inigo's neck. I could see dark rivulet's of blood sliding down his neck. Not good.

Dusting the thing would be easy. It was so focused on Inigo, I was pretty sure the vampire didn't even know I was there. Unfortunately, killing it was out of the question. At least for now.

I grabbed the back of the vamp's shirt and tried to heave it off Inigo. All I succeeded in doing was ripping its shirt half off. Great. Now what?

I had some great abilities, like speed, strength, and fast healing, but none of those would be likely to get it to answer questions.

So I did the only thing left. I pulled my UV gun out and shot it in the leg. The vamp ripped its teeth out of Inigo's throat and reared back, howling in agony.

A UV gun is totally harmless to humans. Well, except maybe that whole skin cancer thing. But a concentrated blast of UV light to the heart will dust a vamp. Heck, a long enough blast anywhere on the torso will put it out of its misery pretty darn quick. An extremity shot, on the other hand, will mostly just hurt it. Badly.

Hurt or not, the vampire didn't let go of Inigo. Instead it lunged for his throat again, no doubt hoping for the healing power of the blood.

I shot it in the other leg.

The vamp dropped to the floor like a sack of potatoes, screaming and cussing and carrying on. It squirmed a bit, but with both its legs useless, it wasn't going anywhere. Inigo wheeled around, ripping his knife out of its sheath with one hand while clamping the other to his bleeding neck. "You okay?" It was hard to tell in the dark how bad the wound was.

"I'll be fine."

I wasn't so sure about that. Unlike me, he wasn't immune to whatever virus it was that turned a person into a vampire. Although Inigo was related to Kabita, he wasn't a hunter. A wound like that could kill him. Or worse, turn him.

Dread pooled in my stomach. I opened my mouth.

"I said I'll be fine," he snapped. "Now let's deal with the vamp, okay?"

The vampire was still screaming and cussing, using words even I'd never heard before. And believe me, I can cuss like a sailor when I put my mind to it.

"Will you shut up already? You're not going to die. They're just a couple of burns."

"You *shot* me," the vamp hissed.

"Uh, yeah. You were trying to turn my friend here into breakfast. Now stop your whining. I've got some questions for you."

"Screw you," the vamp snarled, its eyes glowing a little in the darkness. "I'm not telling you anything."

I glanced over at Inigo, who shrugged. I turned back to the vamp with a little smile. "Well, that's unfortunate." And I shot him in the left knee.

The vamp howled like a banshee. "You bitch!"

"Yes, sometimes that's true." I smiled at the squirming creature. "Now answer my questions, or I keep shooting until you do."

"Fine, fine. What do you want to know?"

"You know a Leprechaun named O'Leery?"

"That cheating scum-sucker?" the vampire shrieked. "Did he put you up to this? I'm going to rip that bastard's head off and suck out his brains. I'm going to…"

"Yeah, I get it," I interrupted before the vamp could really get going. He obviously knew O'Leery. "He claims you stole his pot of gold."

That shut the vamp up. "What the fu— Why would I want his damn gold?"

"You didn't take it then?"

"Hell, no. If I was going to take anything, it would be his cold, black heart. I'd rip it right out of his chest and …"

I pulled the trigger and sent a pure ray of UV light straight through the vampire's own shriveled, black heart. From one blink to the next, he turned to a pile of dust.

"Was that really necessary?"

I turned to Inigo. His neck had stopped bleeding and looked like it was already healing. I guess he must have inherited some of the hunter gene, after all.He was still quite a mess.

"Yeah. Pretty much. You know as well as I do, the minute we left, he'd be off ripping out someone else's throat." Vampires lived for one thing only: to kill and feed. The bloodlust left little room for anything else. They were not sexy. They were not good boyfriend material. They were killing machines.

Inigo sighed and there was an odd sadness in his expression. "I sometimes worry it's getting a little too easy for you, the killing."

I blinked. I had no real answer for that, because sometimes I worried about that, too. But I had a mystery to solve, so I shoved that thought aside for the moment. This was not the time or place to get into a philosophical debate about my life as a hunter.

I changed the subject. "None of the three people O'Leery thought might have his gold even cared about it, let alone took it. What now?"

"I think you need to have another conversation with your client," Inigo said.

***

"Are you calling me a liar?" The Leprechaun's face was

nearly purple with outrage.

"No, Mr. O'Leery," Kabita tried to placate him. "We are simply saying that none of the leads you gave us panned out. None of these people took your gold, so someone else must have. We have to look elsewhere for answers."

That seemed to mollify him slightly. He went from purple to an ordinary red. With a slight huff, he straightened his purple and cream striped waistcoat before sinking into the chair across from Kabita. "Very well, then. What do you need to know?"

"It would be helpful, Mr. O'Leery," I said, "if I could see where your gold was stored. Maybe it will give me a sense of who might have taken it."

His eyes narrowed. "A Leprechaun never gives away his hiding place."

"Please, Mr. O'Leery. This is important." Gods, could this client be any more difficult?

O'Leery mulled it over, then finally gave a little huff. "Very well. Do you have a computer I can use?"

Kabita and I exchanged looks of bafflement. "Computer?" I asked.

He rolled his eyes. "Naturally. If you want to see where I stored my gold."

Kabita turned her laptop toward O'Leery. He scooped it off the desk and onto his lap. He tapped away at the keyboard before returning the laptop to the desk. The screen showed what looked to be some kind of computer game.

"There. I stored my gold in there."

"In a computer game?" Kabita asked.

O'Leery scowled. "Virtual world."

"You mean it's not a *real* pot of gold?" I said.

"Of course not. This is the 21st century. Do you have your money sitting in piles in your closet? No. You have it stored in a bank. It's all 1s and 0s. We Leprechauns do the same thing, only instead of banks, we have a virtual Tir na nÓg."

I stared at the computer screen, where a little fairy-like creature flitted around a green meadow while a faun played a pan flute. Then I turned and stared at Kabita. She looked about as shell-shocked as I felt. I'd been running around the city looking for a damn pot of gold that had never actually existed. Freaking fantastic.

After I finally got my voice back, and my brain returned to some kind of working order, I turned to our client. "Mr. O'Leery, I think we're going to have to call in an expert."

"How I managed not to strangle the leprechaun— excuse me, Leprechaun—is a miracle of the modern age.

* * *

A few hours later, Kabita and I were standing in a dingy studio apartment near the airport. "I can't believe all this trouble was caused by this one little..." I struggled for the right word as I stared at the inert form of our "perpetrator."

"Geek?" Kabita suggested.

Yeah. The word definitely fit. Or maybe... "Nerd?"

Kabita nodded. "Could go either way. Though the sci-fi stuff says 'geek' to me."

"Hey! I like sci-fi."

She gave me a look that clearly said "geek." I guess if the shoe fit.

We both stared at the kid slumped over the keyboard, snoring lightly. He was slightly pudgy and wore a stained Star Wars T-shirt. His glasses had been knocked slightly askew when Kabita put the magical whammy on him. "Is he going to be okay?"

"He'll be fine. I just knocked him unconscious for a bit."

This was the cause of all our trouble. A technogeek game-boy hacker who'd stolen a Leprechaun's pot of gold completely by accident.

Once we'd figured out the pot of gold was virtual, not literal, we'd had Inigo trace the hack back to someone named Eugene Filps. With a name like that, it was no wonder he'd turned hacker. Fortunately for us, he wasn't a very good one.

Apparently good old Eugene had accidently stumbled on the Leprechaun's virtual world and mistaken it for a new computer game. When he'd tried to download a copy of the game for himself, he'd somehow managed to steal O'Leery's virtual pot of gold instead.

Don't ask me how he did it. I had no idea. But Eugene Filps had to be quite possibly the worst hacker ever. Once Inigo had traced him, Kabita and I paid Eugene a little visit. And once Eugene was unconscious, Inigo had hacked the hacker and gotten the gold back.

"What do we do with him?" I glanced down at the gently snoring Eugene. "We can't just leave him like this. And what if he tries it again?"

"Oh, I've got that covered." Kabita smiled and mumbled a few words in what sounded like Spanish before sprinkling blue powder over Eugene's head.

"There. He won't remember a thing when he wakes up, and since Inigo has wiped his system, he'll spend all his time trying to get World of Warcraft back."

That made me laugh. "Good. Let's get out of here. This place smells like stale pizza."

Back at the office, O'Leery was effusive in his thanks. "I can grant you three wishes, if you like." He beamed at me, as though eagerly awaiting my wish for world peace or a tub of Ben & Jerry's.

Three wishes from a Leprechaun. What could possibly go wrong with that? "Uh, thanks, but no thanks."

He shrugged. "Very well. Miss Jones?" He turned to Kabita. "Three wishes for you? As payment for finding my gold?"

"Oh, Mr. O'Leery," Kabita said with that sugary sweet expression I knew far too well. "That is so kind of you. But I only take payment in cold, hard cash."

Once O'Leery had paid his bill—and not with virtual gold, but actual US dollars—and was firmly out of earshot, I turned to Kabita. "Let's make a deal. No more Leprechauns."

She laughed. "Sounds good to me. Listen, Kell's has a live band tonight. Clear over from Ireland. Buy you a Guinness."

I grinned. "Deal."

The End

Want to read more about Morgan's adventures as a vampire hunter? Check out the international bestselling book that started it all: *Kissed by Darkness (Sunwalker Saga – Book 1).*

A Note From Shéa MacLeod

Thank you for reading Kissed by Blood. If you enjoyed this book, I'd appreciate it if you'd help others find it so they can enjoy it too.

Please return to the site where you purchased this book and leave a review to let other potential readers know what you liked or didn't like about Kissed by Blood.

Book updates can be found at www.sheamacleod.com

Be sure to sign up for my mailing list so you don't miss out!
http://sheamacleod.com/mailing-list-2/

You can follow Shéa MacLeod on Facebook https://www.facebook.com/shea.macleod or on Twitter under @Shea_MacLeod.

Shéa MacLeod

[ ]

About Shéa MacLeod

Shéa MacLeod is the author of urban fantasy, post-apocalyptic, scifi, paranormal romances with a twist of steampunk. She also dabbles in contemporary romances with a splash of humor. She resides in the leafy green hills outside Portland, Oregon where she indulges in her fondness for strong coffee, Ancient Aliens reruns, lemon curd, and dragons.

Because everything's better with dragons.

Shéa MacLeod

Other Books by Shea Shéa MacLeod

Made in the USA
San Bernardino, CA
03 April 2016